The Darkness That Bleeds

(Lazarus Sharp)

Prologue

When we leave man to his own devices, can we truly consider him good?

Can he uphold this 'morality' that mankind has constructed?

Indeed, what is evil but a fool's interpretation of tragedy?

Truly, one cannot simply brandish these titles 'good' and 'evil' without understanding that it is all a mere illusion. Why adhere to the bond of man's arrogance and self-righteousness?

This story is the account of one simpleton's plights, the tale of a young man who must face the bonds of man. In the ever-twisting fate of mankind, what will he choose? Will he succumb to man's own hubris, or will he move beyond such constructs?

What would you choose?

After all, are *you* not the one to decide your own fate?

Chapter 1

A rotating fan sat spinning ever so gently, the swift breeze of cool air brushing across the young man's face. His eyes clenched together in between blinking in and out of coherency, the beat of the fan's rhythmic noise becoming more audible with every passing second.

His consciousness began awakening from what appeared to be an incredibly deep slumber.

He finally opened his eyes, taking in his surroundings bit by bit, gazing at cold steel bars.

They wore a backdrop of white, fashioned upright, with each bar only a few inches apart from the next. This cage had such an intricate design that its purpose could very well have been to entrap a wild beast of some sort or at the very least, imprison a few men of ample size.

Whoever or whatever was secured within it, would have no chance of escaping.

His thoughts were those of astonishment and confusion as he examined the structure.

This cage was a work of art, obviously fabricated by a fine craftsman.

Outside of it was nothing but pure light, as though everything beyond the bars and within the whole room was devoid of any color— an eternal abyss of white as far as the eye could see.

A peculiar sensation was festering upon his body. To a degree, his wrists were mobile yet constrained. His ankles *felt* free yet were snug and grasped firmly. His thoughts wavered from curiosity to a creeping hostility. He couldn't move, only able to squirm and struggle like a feeble toddler helpless against forces unknown, as though wrapped in some giant cocoon.

His mind slowly adjusted to the reality in which he presently found himself.

It was now clear that he was caged—moreover, that someone had strapped him to a bed within a cage. That was the truth of it. He tried to recall what had been the catalyst that brought him into his current predicament but alas, he drew a solid blank.

There was nothing but a feeling of emptiness. *Why am I trapped here? Where am I? Who am I, even?* All these questions with no answers. After a few seconds of disbelief and self-doubt, a crackling surge of pain and discomfort pressed sharply against his forehead, the pain shooting deep inside his skull. Slowly but steadily, the throbbing pain and discomfort increased within his head until it became sheer agony just to process a single thought.

It became so intense, it felt as though someone or something had rammed a blunt object across his face with a force so great that he began theorizing that whatever it was, it must have beaten the memories right out of him. And for good measure, it was about to do the same again, just to make sure the hammering beat any recollections right out of him.

It was impossible to recall a single past thought, especially now with this excruciating pain.

For a time, the pain was relentless but after a while of suffering, it was becoming manageable, more or less, appearing to be easing slightly.

Maybe he was growing accustomed to the pain or hopefully, it was slowly subsiding. Either way, it wasn't increasing, so that was a small consolation.

A clicking noise sounded across the room, making his ears perk up. Like a sign of divine providence, the rays of light dissipating, unveiling the walls previously shrouded in the light. From what he could see, the room itself was pretty standard. Four walls, a rotating fan and a few lights sprawled across the ceiling; they were all extinguished.

Yet, the young man felt a bit off and upon closer inspection, as he rotated his head every which way he could, he determined that no doors or windows were visible.

Trapped in a box within a metal box, he laughed to himself, nervous.

The walls themselves were aligned and appeared constructed from cement blocks.

"Hello? Hello? Is anyone here?" the young man cried out. His mouth was dry and raspy, his words only able to reach out to those who would embrace him. Again and again, he attempted to yell and beckon but his voice was stale and lacked vigor. He kept calling out to anyone willing to listen, almost begging for at least an acknowledgement of his existence.

At this point, he'd have been willing to have anyone help him, or even just to answer his calls for help. He just needed someone, anyone. After a long while of hollering and subsequent coughing due to his pathetic cries, he then accepted defeat.

He was wasting his precious and slow-declining energy, truly possessing no other option but to merely lie still, staring at the fan swinging counterclockwise. After what seemed like a millennium to the young man, a voice called out, "Hello, child. Confused, are we?"

Was that a voice, or just his mind playing some uncalled-for games?

Regardless, he was stunned and utterly relieved to hear another voice instead of his own pathetic howling. Hopefully, someone had answered his hopes and with all the strength he could muster, the young man broke the silence with a high-pitched squeal of desperation.

"Hello! Help me! Please, help me! Get me out of here, please! I'm begging you," he shouted, waiting for the reply. "Please, help me!"

"That is entirely up to you, my child. Will you *let* me help you?" the voice replied in turn and the young man's eyes teared up.

"Yes! Yes, of course, I will let you help me," he said.

"Then so shall it be done. My nurse, Sevant, will be there shortly, Adam."

The young man's unease was fading away ever so slightly now. His name was Adam and he had an identity, the proof that his existence had meaning even if it served only a minute purpose in the grand scheme of things. Shortly after the voice had silenced, Adam could hear the pitter-pattering of what had to be footsteps, rushed yet concise and with a goal in mind.

Yes, salvation was on its way and a small feeble smile ran across Adam's face. Was he to be free at last? Would he learn the where, why, and how?

These thoughts rang through his head as the anticipation became almost unbearable.

The wall was making a low humming noise followed by the sound of locks releasing and bare metal surfaces scraping against each other. Abruptly, a cool breeze flowed through from an appearing crack within the wall, the sensation skimming across his bare toes and ending on his dry lips. "Remain calm and quiet," a dull raspy voice said.

Being strapped to the bed limited Adam's movement, preventing him fully taking in the figure of the mysterious male. Adam waited, apprehensive.

Keys jingled and the door to the cage swung open with a loud clanking.

Finally, they made eye contact. Old, ragged, yet as tall as a beanstalk.

"Well, I hear you're in need of food and water. Am I to assume that is correct, Mr. Adam?" the figure said coldly.

"Yes, but I'd first like to get out of this bed here. I've been trapped in here for so long, strapped in this position for I don't know how long, so please let me free," he said yearning to be set loose. Immediately, he could feel the restraints release their powerful grip; an instant wave of emotion set in with the predominant one being that of gratitude.

"Thank you! Thank you so much!" he exclaimed, carefully arising and clutching at his wrists. Adam then reached forward, gingerly stretching out his back and sitting upright on the bed.

Twisting his torso to the left and then the right, he made the point of getting a better look at his savior's physique. The face was as normal as any, a pale complexion yet with dark brown piercing eyes. But as Adam looked at his arms and torso, his gratitude slowly shifted to fear, the likes of which he'd never felt before.

"What the…" Adam said, noticing a decapitated cow's head hanging from its matted hide, lying across the gentleman's bloody hands.

"Ah yes, this. I forgot to mention that this head here is your dinner. You see, this facility is not well known across the world. Devoid of any prying eyes with their... constrictions.

"As such, we have a sustainable form of production of vegetables, dairy, and as you see here, meat. Due to extenuating circumstances, we have been running low on supplies. Waste not, want not. Am I right?" the man said, blood dripping across the plain floor, forming a small puddle.

Adam looked at the man with disgust and horror.

"What's wrong with you?" Adam said.

Ignoring the comment, the man continued.

"Just this morning, this poor sap's time was up. We needed the calories and this thing needed too much upkeep, so…" he said, sliding a finger of his free hand across his neck.

The man placed the head onto a nearby table.

Reaching into one of the drawers beneath the table, the man removed a cleaver and without notice or any other prior warning, began pounding away at the cow's head.

All the while, Adam stared into its dead eyes.

"So, since you are hungry and all, you might as well wash this down with some ice-cold water," the man said as he continued hacking away at the head, the sound of snapping bone and flesh permeating the room, and spatters of blood spraying across Adam's face.

"See, maybe you know this already," he went on. "But in some countries, cow head is considered a delicacy. Well, it's the brain actually. But, to remove the brain, you have to hack away at the head just like trying to get to the juicy middle of a coconut. And let's not forget, bones have a nice amount of calcium, and the hair and hide are great for cleaning one's colon."

The nose and eyes were melding with the rest of the chopped-up flesh, the tongue also long since diced into pieces.

The man was relentless, swinging away at the carcass as if it gave him a sense of euphoria.

"You know, if you think about it, it's simply poetic. The needs of the many outweigh those of the few. Yet why is that? Why do *we* believe that?"

"Please, enough!" Adam said, begging him to stop but the man was far from done.

"Now, now, now. We wouldn't want you to choke on a bone now, would we?"

After what seemed like hours, Adam was still lying in the bed, pushing his face against the pillow. "All done!" the man said in contentment. "Come on. Up you get," he added, grasping Adam's head and reeling him up from the bed as if he were a root in the earth.

The blood was soaking into his hair.

"Bon appetit," the man said, placing in front of Adam a pile of mush and a glass of water. Quickly, Adam drank from the glass and finally felt a tad refreshed.

How long have I been without water? he thought.

Handing Adam a spoon, the man spoke. "Now, here's the deal. You either eat a good amount of this pile of shit I just made or…" He paused and pointed to the mangled flesh. "Or I'll be doing that to your slimy little face. Oh, and you have fifteen minutes."

Leaving the cage and locking the door behind him, he continued to the separating wall before turning back. "You know, sometimes, life can weigh a person down, so maybe it wouldn't be so bad if you let me have my fun?"

The sheet of white came back into the picture. The room had no openings beyond the section Sevant had left and even if he could open it, he still had the cage to deal with. With the threat of a cleaver slicing down his face, Adam was in utter shock. Mere moments ago, he hadn't been able to recall his past. He knew no one in this facility, and as soon as he thought he would escape this confusion, he found himself in a nightmare. Walking to and fro, Adam contemplated.

"Think, think, think," he whispered. "Who am I? What is this place? And most importantly, how the hell do I get out of here?" Adam's thoughts trailed off and one question seemed to lead to another. He simply couldn't collect his thoughts no matter how hard he tried.

His mind was faltering, leading to frustration and soon, to anger. Grasping the bars to the cage, Adam shook them with ferocity, screaming, "Get me the hell out of here!"

He swung his arms about and kicked the bars, his freedom barred, with no escape in sight.

After a few minutes of his pointless struggle, the sharp sound of a screeching speaker rang through Adam's ears. "Is there a problem, Adam?"

It was that same voice, the first voice Adam had heard. The same voice that named him, and the very same voice that quelled his fears however fleeting that feeling had been.

"I don't want to die! I need to leave this place!" Adam screeched.

"Why do you need to leave this place? Is there any place that you can think of besides your own little cell?" the voice said with a hint of humorous intent.

"No, I don't remember a thing, but I can't stay here like this! You sent a deranged lunatic to help me, yet all he did was chop up an animal's face in front of my very eyes! Yes, he hacked at the head with a cleaver. Then on top of that, he threatened to kill me in fifteen minutes! What kind of help is that? So, yes, I really want to leave this place."

"Now, now, Adam. How dare you beg for my assistance and in the very same breath, spit in my face! You fool, were you not released from your restraints? Did you not receive fluids to help refresh that ungrateful little throat of yours? If one of my men expects a little gratitude, so be it, you pathetic little worm!" the voice explained with more authority.

"Gratitude? My *life* is beyond any gulp of water and being slightly less uncomfortable!"

"Why? Why do you think your life should be any more important than the glass of water, eh? What makes you think that there are these invisible lines of values?

"Your self-preservation is merely an instinct and if you blindly follow those instincts, you're no more than a monkey. Reality is so much more complex, and I have no qualms about letting you rot in that cell. However, if you cooperate and follow my instructions exactly as I relay them to you, you will live another day! You are my monkey, and I am your master.

"You will never call out to me again. You will not speak unless I ask you to, and you will never attempt to go near your bars again, understood? It's up to you. But please be warned.

"Fail to comply, and I will have Sevant reenter your humble little abode and rip your entrails out while you watch," the voice said with cold condemnation. "Do I make myself clear?"

Adam could barely utter a word but in a subservient fashion, planted his knees on the ground.

"Good, now five minutes have already passed, so I suggest you eat as much as you can. Sevant has very few hobbies, so it would be best if you were not to see one of the few things he enjoys." The voice's words felt as if its authority was absolute, and the consequences of straying from them dire. Walking to the bed, Adam slumped his shoulders, confused, scared, and alone.

All he had were his thoughts, thinking about the many scenarios in which Sevant would feed his destructive nature upon him. Trembling, he grabbed the spoon, barely able to keep it steady as he shoveled out a piece of mangled flesh.

Then, with much revulsion, he placed the mush into his mouth. Hair, blood and marrow mangled through his lips, across his tongue slithering, disgusting slime.

The sensation was completely revolting.

Pressing his hands against his mouth, Adam swung his head back and forth.

If he were to let go, the contents would have splattered across the floor. The blood gushed across his tongue while hair and hide matted against his teeth, the chunks of bone sliding down his throat, jabbing his insides as they slid down even further into his stomach.

Tears streamed down his face as each bite made Adam come closer to vomiting.

But he could not give in to it, of course; if he did, then Sevant would find this a justifiable offense to satisfy his 'hobby.' No, Adam would not die like this. He refused to.

He refused to just lie there and die helpless and feeble. If that meant becoming a monkey for the voice, then so be it, because when he had the chance, he would escape this hell on earth.

Still eating and becoming accustomed to the putrid flesh, the wall slid across and sure enough, there stood Sevant, gazing at Adam and he began a slow clap.

"Bravo! Well done! I'm impressed. You've been eating that sludge for over thirty minutes and it looks like you're almost done!" Perplexed, Adam simply became silent.

He was remembering the voice's words not to speak unless told to do so.

"What a wise lad. So you've decided to play ball? Perfect, but I'm a tad disappointed really. You see, I'd have thought by now, you would have upchucked that garbage. In which case, it would have been game over for you, but I'm a man of my own word, so I won't pound a cleaver on your face anytime soon," Sevant said with a smirk. "I saw you eating and after the fifteen minutes were up, me and the boys just wanted to know how long you'd keep it up!"

Sevant set off laughing

"We had a bit of a bet going. I mean, yeesh. Who wants to live that badly in the first place! Honestly, it was priceless. Me and the other attendants started placing bets. Good God, it was such a fortunate thing that I started rooting for you. You not only gave me some good laughs, which in this place are few and far between, but you also made my wallet a bit heavier. Fair play to you, lad."

Adam's blood began to boil but he retained his composure.

"So, since you've been cooperative minus that little outburst you had earlier, I'll go get your *actual* rations." Sliding through the entrance were two little carts not more than four feet high, one with basic cleaning supplies, a trash bin and even small hygienic products, while the other had a few edibles—a loaf of bread, a stick of butter, a cup of honey, sweet baby carrots and to top it all off, a cold glass of milk. The steam rising from the carrots started to drift into Adam's nostrils. Even stale bread and water would have been a Godsend, but this was saliva-inducing.

This was the smell of something edible and fresh.

Opening the cage once more, Sevant was still smirking and proceeded to wheel in the carts, wiping down the entire cell. He removed blood and gore, hair, hide and crushed bone from the table and floor, before vigorously scrubbing clean the more stubborn areas.

After a short time, a glimmer of white peeked through, the room slowly returning to some sort of normality, no doubt in preparation for the next unfortunate soul.

"Go ahead, eat. I don't care whether you're done or not; once this cell is up to *his* standards, I'll be taking my leave including the food." Yet as Sevant looked back, he saw nothing more than a starved animal stuffing its gullet relentlessly.

The carrots were the first to go. No more than two handfuls and they were gone.

The honey, he poured directly onto the bread with one hand while he held the stick of butter in the other. The savory delight of butter and the candy-like sweetness of the honey began warming his soul as if the last few hours were nothing more than a nightmare from which he had awoken. Licking the plates clean, he finally downed the cold, creamy beverage.

In fewer than a few twitches of his eyes, it was gone.

"Man, you're disgusting! I get it. You were hungry, but I would have thought that eating nearly half a cow's head would have made you full or at least make you lose your appetite. How wrong was I?"

It was true. Adam's stomach felt as if it would burst but the fear and anxiety had done more to compensate for his ravenous appetite.

And for a few moments, he forgot he was a captive hanging onto hopes of survival.

"Take these pills," Sevant ordered, passing him a glass of water and what appeared to be a medicinal substance. Adam drank them both and Sevant's eyes gleamed.

"This is going to be fun, I can tell," Sevant said with a menacing grin, raising his hands high. "Welcome, Adam! Welcome to everlasting hell until your inevitable death!"

Adam's eyes widened and tears were forming once again due to the sheer horror.

Sevant finished his cleaning and stepped away from the cell. He locked up, exiting through the separating wall. All the while, Adam stood, gripping the bars tightly and staring in the direction of the exit. Letting go of the bars in haste, he realized the small error he'd made.

He shuffled to his bed and lay there staring at the rotating fan once again. Thankfully, his restraints were off; however, he was clearly not free. His mind was contemplating his fate.

His name was Adam, but why was this all he knew about himself? His life before this nightmare was a complete blur as if he had never existed, as if he'd been born on this day and knew nothing about his past. The light within the room was fading away as if signaling the end of the day. The end of his first day as Adam. Or was it?

His ever-growing fall to insanity began to fester on this very day.

***

When man experiences agony, there are those who succumb and those who overcome. There's really no happy medium. However, a select few move way beyond failure or victory, those select few finding the real answer. It matters not whether you prevail in anything.

It matters not if you lose in anything, either.

To live or to die is a lie, you see. The select few realize that we are all nothing, and that nothingness is the true answer, the ever-expanding void of the universe simply growing and growing. Man is but a flicker in an already extinguished flame.

Life? There is no such thing, for man always returns to the earth. We merely gasp for a breath of air for a few moments and then the void of the world reaches out her warm embrace.

Chapter 2

"Adam, wakey wakey, hands off snakey!" Rising from his bed, Adam awoke to see Sevant fiddling with keys, attempting to open the cage. "So, today is a pretty special day, shit for brains," Sevant explained. "We are going on a little field trip. Come on, out you come."

The cage door opened, and someone had shifted the wall.

Confused yet eager, Adam simply did as Sevant told him.

He found speaking could lead to worse encounters, so he was adamant he would remain silent until spoken to. Sevant's expression wore a smirk.

"So, obedient today, are we?" said Sevant, slowly clenching his fingers into a fist and raising it above his head. "Don't you want one of these? I really can't wait till you fall out of line."

He chuckled, looking at his fist. Adam just continued his silence, walking out of his cage and finally taking a step out toward the light radiating from the outer wall, just to find a long narrow hallway. Nothing but the color white, devoid of doors and appearing to be an endless chasm.

"What's the matter? Not much to see?" Sevant said with sarcasm. "All the other patients have their own cell block within these walls and the only way to tell is to look for a fingerprint scanner." Adam was finally understanding.

This place was certainly not the norm; even though he could not recollect much, he still knew that the outside world had more color to it than this.

"I guess I should explain a little further since I'm the only one who seems to be talking here," Sevant said.

"Sorry, I—"

Before he could even finish his sentence, Adam's face contorted as a fist melded into his face like the force of a waterfall crashing down upon him. He fell to the ground dazed and confused.

"Hey, numbskull, didn't you remember what I told you? You don't speak, you don't eat, you don't even take a shit unless told to do so, right? Do we understand one another?"

Sevant's face beamed with joy and appeared relieved to have had a reason to thump hell out of his captive. "Truth be told, I just needed to blow off some steam, and you were just *wayyy* too obedient at the get go. Please, do feel free to grow a pair of balls once in a while, so I can beat you senseless from time to time. Getting a good ass kicking now and again builds character, don't you agree?" Adam's eyes were burning with rage, but he returned to his silence.

"Hmm, well I'll be damned. You're no fun," Sevant said. "As I was saying before I was so rudely interrupted, each patient's cell block is just like yours. They're all the same.

"White room, no visible forms of exits since the walls slide in and out and finally, the big birdcages as I like to call them, each one decorated with a bed and a piss bucket.

"Oh, and just so you know, no one else can open a wall unless the fingerprint matches that of the prescribed nurse. So, basically, if you ever have the urge to step outside and go for a walk, you might wanna start kissing my ass from time to time. Not even the doctor comes in.

"He really loves to keep his subjects devoid of any distractions except for their tests. Oops, too much info. Come along now."

As Sevant moved forward, Adam's eyes were noticing the fingerprint scanners along the walls. Every twenty or so steps, he would see another scanner attached to the wall, counting seven in total by the time they had reached an actual door.

"Come on in. Come on. Over here, mister shit for brains."

After fiddling with some keys in his back pocket, Sevant opened the door to reveal another sheet of white, yet full of some kind of color on this occasion. The color brown, perhaps?

Yes, Adam recalled such a color existing far beyond this place.

Within the room, square cardboard boxes stacked upon one another, forming an even bigger square, and there were a couple of white drawers and a megaphone, of all things.

At the end of the room, another door.

Adam glanced around, but then the megaphone screeched something aloud.

"All these boxes must be opened before the allotted time of five minutes is up," said the voice coming through the megaphone. "If you refuse, or if you fail, I will have your nurse reprimand you."

"I'm looking forward to this, shit for brains," said Sevant.

"If even one single box is left unopened, or even partly opened within the allotted time, Sevant will be instructed to give you a penalty shock."

Sevant eagerly walked to one of the drawers and pulled out a shiny metal rod with prongs sticking from the top. Sweat was forming on Adam's face and body, pooling in the small of his back, making him itch. He focused in on what other demands the voice had in store for him.

"If you open all the boxes within the allotted time frame of five minutes, you will proceed to the next door. That is all, and your time begins… now."

Five minutes to open what seemed to be dozens of boxes.

Adam grabbed a box and attempted to open it. It was noticeably light, almost as if empty, but it was taped shut and his fingers kept prying into its sides ferociously.

Adam kept clawing away until at last, it opened.

Empty. He immediately went after another and another, each a void just like the last.

His fingers were aching now.

"Two-minute warning, cunt muffin," yelled Sevant.

Adam's eyes were tearing yet again.

This task is impossible, he thought. *How can anyone open all these boxes within the time frame with their bare hands? Just not do-able.*

In an instant, Adam's mind flashed, looking to one of the drawers. Could there be something in there to help with this task? The drawer from which Sevant had pulled the electrical rod may well contain torture devices, but what about the other?

Sevant's cheery face faded just as abruptly when Adam's eyes locked onto the drawer.

"Time is up. Adam, please stop what you're doing," the voice said.

Sevant seemed relieved and regained his composure.

"Well, I'm only allowed one measly shock, is that correct, Doc?"

"Yes," the voice answered. Adam waited for the voice to say more, but it never came.

It never mentioned how long Adam would need to remain in this room, and for how long Sevant would subject him to this torture.

Adam instinctively ran toward the door, flailing about with all his strength, pulling the handle in clear desperation, but the door would not budge as if to capitalize on the fact of his failure. Like a lion pouncing onto its prey, Sevant wrestled Adam to the ground.

"Looks like this falls into the category of an offense, due for a reprimanding!"

Adam's strength had already started to wane, his arms and legs mere twigs in comparison to Sevant's hulking mass of muscle. His fists thumped down on Adam's abdomen over and over until he heaved and threatened to puke. At this point, Sevant stopped and waited for Adam to finish. All the food that Adam had eaten the night prior now spread across the ground in a steaming, chunky pool. Adam could even see the cow's eyeball he had ingested as well.

"Why are you fucking doing this to me?" Adam said, Sevant's foot coming crashing against his lower jaw, breaking his speech.

"Because we can and since you're well enough to speak, I don't mind if I do."

The sensation of cold yet sharp metal stabbed into Adam's leg and in nanoseconds, the shock was jolting through his body, causing his teeth to grit.

His eyes slowly rolled to the back of his head, showing only their whites.

All his sensations became one as if the pain transcended into sight, hearing, and taste. As he convulsed on the floor, feeling the electricity attacking every square inch of his body, Adam's mind cracked until in the end, all that remained to sense was darkness. Forcing his eyes open, the endless sheen of white was comforting. For a few moments, he lost himself in deep thought staring at the ceiling, the fan still rotating to the hum of relative silence.

He couldn't help but think about those steamed baby carrots and sweetbreads.

What a waste, he thought as his belly growled without apology.

Then, abruptly, the voice spoke.

"You failed your first test; therefore, it seems an appropriate time for me to explain to you your predicament. You may take the same test as many times as necessary until you successfully complete it. However, each failure in turn has an increase of one added penalty such as this test's penalty shock. So, each test has a different penalty for failure, and the more times you fail, the more… Well, need I go on? I think you understand how it works. Success, Adam. I need you to succeed so I can carry out further tests. So, it's in both our interests that you pass each test."

Adam's mind traveled to that moment. The moment where he was completely powerless against Sevant, recognizing how weak he felt in comparison. "Your next test will begin in a few hours. Sevant shall be serving you your rations before too long. That is all."

Adam rose from his bed, stretching out his limbs.

His entire body felt sore, and his head ached. When his eyes adjusted to the light, he saw new amenities within his room: a sink, a portable toilet and a small chair and table all sat beside his bed. Adam hadn't seen furniture like this in such a long time.

Strange, he thought. *How can it be that I haven't seen a simple toilet in years?*

Attempting to assemble his broken memories, all Adam remembered was waking up in this place, almost as if he'd been born here. However, deep down within the core of his soul, he knew he'd lived in the outside world beforehand.

How long has it been since I've seen the light of day?

The wall separated and out popped Sevant, bringing in what appeared to be a tray of food. "Looks like you couldn't be as obedient as you thought. Pathetic!" Sevant chuckled. "You should have seen your face as you scrambled to open the door. You made my day, yesterday.

"I feel like a new man now. Honestly, I haven't had this much fun with a patient in a while. They typically fail the pretest and throw up. Don't get me wrong, butchering someone's face is all well and good, but it's too messy and short lived. A beating, however, is different. It's art.

"Every strike and blow I dealt is present on your body. Every scar, every bruise, every sprain paints a beautiful picture. Once you heal again, you'll be a blank canvas and I can start again.

"That is if you can even make it to the healing process." Sevant chuckled again. "Well, I guess it's a good thing you don't have a mirror because you look like a swollen grape. A battered grape. All my punches and kicks are gonna get harder from now on, so you can look out.

"I've been holding back of course, all for your own sake. Ain't I a nice guy?"

Adam started to feel something, or rather, he felt the lack of something. It was numbness within his grief-stricken heart, as if the man's threats were losing their weight.

Not as afraid as before, he spoke out.

"If you keep beating me, won't I die? Then, all your fun will end. Haven't you thought of that? What enjoyment would you have if I were to die?"

"Hey! Did I say you could speak, cunt muffin?"

Adam's face flew to his right shoulder as quick as lightning. Sevant's open-palmed hand had made its mark on him, leaving a pinkish hue to his skin.

"No, you didn't, but if you're having fun with me, it would be a waste to just kill me, wouldn't it?"

Spitting on Adam's face, Sevant looked at him in disgust. "Well, go on," he said reluctantly.

"How does this work? Why kill people just because they can't eat a dead carcass? Why am I even here to begin with?" Adam asked. "What's the point supposed to be?"

"Because it's a test," said Sevant. "To see whether or not the patient's survival instincts are strong enough to cope with the stress provided. It's not always the same test, and it varies on difficulty. It depends on his mood."

"Whose mood?" asked Adam.

Sevant looked at him coldly, slow to unlock the cage door, yet quick to change the subject.

"Just to let you know, you pissed yourself yesterday like a squealing baby. Had to change your clothes and hose down your disgusting little body for sanitation purposes."

Adam fell back into silence. It was clear Sevant could not be reasoned with, being way too busy enjoying the agony of others.

"Here's your slop." Sevant dropped the tray on the desk and simply left Adam, locking the gate behind him and walking past the sliding wall.

Finally, when he found himself alone, Adam walked over toward the desk to see what he would eat today. A glass of water, a bowl of oatmeal. A green apple. Adam savored every bite. It was the only thing he could look forward to in this hell.

What more can I do?

Thinking back on the test, it seemed impossible to achieve but if he had a sharp object like a knife of some sort, he could just slice open the tape sealing the empty boxes, possibly cutting the time in half. That drawer Sevant had opened must have had other things inside of it—maybe even a tool that he could use to pass the test.

Sevant's face changed the second Adam locked eyes on it.

But it didn't add up; what did Sevant have to lose if Adam found anything that would help him pass the test? Was he simply upset that he wouldn't have the permission to shock him?

Or was there more at stake than Adam had realized?

Adam stood, pacing around the room. *What can I do?*

If he didn't pass the test, Sevant would just beat him up again. He wasn't confident that he would be able to pass the test today, so he needed to make a gamble.

He needed to think of something. The voice clearly said that he'd be taking the same test. Every time the doctor spoke, his words were precise and filled with authority.

If Adam were to interpret everything the voice said in a clear and literal sense, then these tests would be consistent and orderly in nature.

Sevant would always be watching over him waiting for the moment he failed, and the beatings would continue. Adam embarked on a plan of action.

First things first. I need to get stronger. Assuming I fail twice or maybe three times in a row, I need to be able to hold my own against Sevant in the long run.

Even if I do pass the test, Sevant will most likely be there for the next one. Might as well put on some muscle to cushion his attacks, and to make his attacks less straightforward for him.

Adam plopped himself chest down onto the cold floor, propelling himself up and down against the stone slabs. *Push-ups. These are called push-ups.* He remembered these as a kid in the gym. Like a spark of lightning, Adam finally regained some of his memory.

"Right, school. What school did I go to?" After a while of losing himself in thought while doing his push-ups, Adam gave up to focus on his plan.

Getting stronger wouldn't happen in an instant. It might be months before he may be able to even pose a threat to Sevant. *So how will I lighten the load of the beatings? Sevant's beatings?*

Nothing came to mind. Everything Adam did, even breathing, agitated Sevant.

Just by existing, he irritated the hell out of Sevant.

Abruptly, Adam felt resistance; forty push-ups were his max. For now, he simply knelt and did half push-ups which weren't as punishing, but at least he was continuing. After thirty more or so, he was exhausted. His arms were burning, and he now knew how weak he really was.

He may not have been scrawny, but he was out of shape. Well, at least he had made a start.

Slamming into his bed, Adam kept thinking of ways to avoid serious injury. *If only I were a turtle.* Yet again, more nomenclature and basic knowledge began flooding into Adam's mind. *I could just find the corner of a room and assume the fetal position.*

However pathetic or degrading it might be, at least he might spare a few bones from breaking. Adam steeled his will and made a goal. He would take the test today and fail, that was a given. But upon the third attempt, he would pass with flying colors.

He regained his composure, jogging in place, raising his knees to his waist height.

After a few hours of jogging, push-ups, sit-ups and taking a nap, the wall slid open.

"Hellooo, shit for brains! Let's go out and have some fun, shall we?"

"Yeah, why not? Let's go have some fun," said Adam with a crooked smile.

This time, he was not faking it. Adam had a plan, and the plan made a world of difference!

Shortly after opening the cage, Sevant swung at Adam.

But this time, Adam was ready, accepting the blow with his right arm, blocking most of the damage. Sevant saw the resolve and anger in Adam's eyes.

"Oh, so you grew a pair, huh, mister tough guy? Let's see how long it takes for them to shrivel up and turn into tiny raisins." Adam once again walked out of his cell, following Sevant through the hallway. As they passed the fingerprint scanners, he noticed one was emitting a flashing green light. Adam stopped, staring at the peculiar sight.

Sevant trailed back; Adam was no longer in his line of sight.

"First of all, get the fuck back here." Grabbing Adam's shirt collar, Sevant whisked him forward like a twig, landing him on the floor rather clumsily.

Adam got up, dusted himself off, and walked toward the door again in an act of defiance.

"We are gonna be late if we don't pick up the pace, you idiot!"

Sevant's demeanor blotched an impatient mottled pink like a can of cheap chopped ham.

Immediately, Sevant rushed toward Adam, yet the puny patient anticipated this.

It was why his fist connected with Sevant's jutting jaw, achieving a most satisfying crunch.

Normally, a hit like this wouldn't even faze a man like Sevant for he was too stubborn to let it. However, right now, his full weight and force were pushing up against Adam's fist, and coupled with Adam's meager strength, the results were somewhat impressive.

It was like a featherweight boxer landing a lucky punch on a heavyweight boxer. Far less power, but the combination of both forces colliding head-on was phenomenal.

This was a small family car careening into a great truck along an interstate, neither of them slowing. Whether by luck or an expertly placed punch, the result was the same, and it boiled down to the fact that Adam had just caught Sevant with the perfect punch in the perfect place.

In that brief skirmish, Adam managed to kick Sevant in the groin and retreated backwards for a bit, then ran headlong toward the testing area, quickly making it toward the end of the hall right in front. The testing area's door was sealed shut. He could not get in.

Feeling like a total fool, he quickly remembered Sevant had used his own fingerprint on the door. The whole point was to buy time and search those Godforsaken drawers.

Not all was lost, however, for *the voice* spoke in a whimsical fashion.

"I don't condone this sheer act of defiance, but you've caught me in a good mood, and I'd like to see how this plays out. Care to see if I'd let you in?"

"Yes please!" The door immediately shifted to the side.

Still dazed and in pain, Sevant began spewing expletive after expletive within the hall.

Adam, now in the testing area, ran toward the drawers and set about inspecting their contents. He saw the electric metal rod, of course, but nothing else. He opened the second drawer and lo and behold, a small pocketknife lay in an otherwise barren compartment.

Grabbing it quickly, he then opened the third and last minuscule drawer—finding it empty.

"So, Sevant's late, is he?"

Ignoring the voice's remark, Adam ran toward the boxes and began slicing them open before the announcement of the allotted time. The voice said nothing.

Adam continued, box after box, opening one after another, able to see the goal coming closer.

The pocketknife made things so much easier, slicing through the packing tape with ease.

"You little shit. Trying to show me up, eh? Well, I'm going to fucking beat you senseless!" Sevant shouted, bursting through the door and sprinting toward Adam.

"The test has already started without your presence, Sevant," *the voice* announced in a loud and more audible sound. Sevant nearly tripped over himself as he attempted to put on the brakes of his initial assault. Then, begrudgingly, he walked over to the drawer, grabbed the metal rod and grit his teeth, staring daggers at Adam. But Adam's mind was, of course, elsewhere.

It was time for action. He wasn't stupid and knew he was no match for Sevant in the shape he was now, and he also knew that the voice was pulling the strings. But this was just his first step of defiance against those who had placed him in here. He planned to fight back.

Now was not a time to admit defeat and lie back, waiting to be trodden down again.

"Two-minute warning," Sevant said. No enthusiasm, no insults, and no *cunt muffin* this time, just calm remarks as if he finally realized he too had a job of his own.

Adam could see only eleven more boxes remained, and he continued cutting through each. He was on a roll, finally able to develop a routine—and it was working, thankfully.

One last box to go. Right before Adam sliced open the latest box in his hands, he noticed Sevant's mood shift, as if he was waiting in anticipation.

He seemed focused, however, waiting for something big to happen. He was primed.

Whether it was intuition or mere luck, Adam inspected the box before he cut it open.

On close inspection, the box was the same as any of the others but the more he flipped and looked at it from every conceivable angle, the more anxious and frustrated Sevant looked.

Finally flipping the box upside down, Adam could see a small note taped to the bottom of the box. 'Whoever opens this box shall die.' Instinctively, and as though he had just primed a grenade, Adam threw the box as far from himself as he could.

He needed to distance himself from the note of death.

"Fuck you!" Sevant screamed.

Adam's intuition and alertness was able to read Sevant's face and mannerisms, avoiding an incredibly dreadful mistake.

"Fuck you, too!" Adam said back with triumph in his voice. After checking all the other boxes, Adam saw nothing out of the ordinary and all the other boxes were devoid of any notes.

"Thirty seconds, shithead." Adam figured out how to beat the test, yet now a bigger wall lay before him. All the boxes had to be opened, yet whoever opened *this* box would die.

Adam's thoughts rushed as he began contemplating how to solve this conundrum.

"Time is up!" the voice announced. "Two penalty shocks will be administered."

Sevant walked toward Adam with a cold, determined stare as if his pride lay on the line.

His thoughts were full of rage because as much as he'd like to rip out Adam's entrails and burn his remains, he could do no such thing without the doctor's permission.

Adam walked slowly back toward a corner of the room.

"Looks like a reprimandable offense!" Sevant said.

"No, not at all. He's merely picked a location for you to administer the penalty. Please proceed with the task. However, there will be no other forms of physical trauma until further notice," the voice said.

"What? Did you not see what just happened earlier in the hallway? Do you have a screw loose, Doc?" Sevant yelled. The resulting silence was abrupt and trailed for a few moments.

Sevant blinked, several beads of sweat forming on his brow, his face slowly turning red from the anxiety.

Am I breaking him? Adam thought.

"Doc! Doc, are you there? Did you hear me?"

"Tread carefully, Sevant. If you speak to me in that tone again, I will place you into solitary confinement again and for twice as long," the doctor said coldly.

"Yes, Doctor, I apologize," Sevant said with the now cold sweat dripping down his neck. "I didn't mean it, honest, sir. I… I'm just angry that the patient attacked me, that's all. And I was waiting on the go ahead from yourself to make him suffer."

"If I may say so, you rely so fervently on emotions, Sevant. They are meaningless in the grand scheme of things, are they not? Whatever the patient has done or will ever do is also a part of the study. Move on from it and simply learn to adapt," said the voice. "Now then, carry on."

Still facing the corner, Adam grabbed onto his knees and prepared himself.

Sevant's face was swelling with anger.

"You've been thinking of ways to deal with this, huh, cunt muffin? Well, guess what, I'll just hold this button down till there is hardly any charge left! Give you the shock of your life!"

The cold steel once again pressed deep into Adam's flesh and this time, Sevant decided it was best for the shock to originate from the base of his neck.

"Penalty shock number one, bitch!" Instantly, the familiar agonizing pain Adam had once felt decided to jog his memory.

The electricity coursed through his body, and he held on for as long as he could but eventually, his arms could not resist the torrent of power and pain.

Flopping like a fish out of water, Adam's eyes rolled to the back of his head, and he was beginning to lose consciousness. Sevant's extremities felt a surge of pleasure and release.

The blood flow in his veins quickened and his primal nature showed.

His eyes became wild, ready to leap from their sockets if they could.

"This is for kicking me in the balls, little bitch! Remember that in future," Sevant said, smiling and pulling the trigger at the same time. Just as Adam's mind was about to go blank from the pain, the shocking abruptly stopped. Slowly, Adam turned around to breathe for a bit.

Yet there was Sevant yet again, showing a sly grin.

"Wakey, wakey. I just wanted to see that pathetic little face squirm!" Sevant proclaimed, giving Adam a cheerful wave.

"Seconds out, round two!"

Jabbing the prongs into Adam's thigh, Sevant plunged as much electricity as the rod could spare. "Penalty shock number two, my friend!" he screeched.

It seemed like an eternity to Adam.

His body's convulsions wouldn't stop until finally, he sullied himself yet again and then nothing. His neck burning, his body aching, Adam arose from bed feeling the urge to vomit all over the white floor, yet the blaring headache becoming more prevalent by the minute distracted him. He'd failed the way he thought he would, but at least he'd survived.

He remembered the ice-cold feeling of death looming over his shoulders when he'd read the note from the bottom of the box earlier that day.

Simply opening all the boxes would have been too easy with the pocketknife. Adam sighed in disappointment. The 'doctor' did not seem the type to make things easy.

Frankly, everything had come at a cost so far.

Does the doctor want to force me to make an almost impossible decision?

What kind of sick game is this? To get past the door, Adam would need to open all the boxes, one of which spelled certain death. Could he really open all the boxes and survive?

Was it a bluff or a poorly crafted joke? No, it couldn't be.

The good doctor wouldn't try something like that, especially after all he had been through, and all the trouble to reinforce how serious he was with his penalties.

Then one of them would most certainly equate to a death wish if he were to open it.

"All the boxes must be opened," Adam whispered to himself, then his eyes widened.

And then he understood. "All the boxes must be opened," he said for the third time out loud. He grinned pitifully, now understanding what the test had been leading up to all along.

He would need to convince Sevant to open the box, and if the doctor was true to his word—which he surely must be—then Sevant would be no more. But then what?

What would come after that?

Chapter 3

Irony is a cruel and vindictive mistress, he thought. At the same time, he knew he was doomed to have endless bouts with insanity and cruelty for the rest of his life. "Why can't I get a break?" he muttered. Within his mindscape, he could see Sevant looking as menacingly as ever, towering over him, lurching forward with his giant hands clasping Adam's neck like a snug collar.

"Do you think you came here just to stand around and chit chat?"

"Sorry, I just can't take much more of this, Sevant, I really can't." Tears welled up in his eyes. Sevant let go of Adam's throat and laughed.

"Oh, but there's so much more to come!"

Within an instant, a spark of creativity came to mind; in fact, there was a glimmer of hope. Adam's mind started piecing together the remnants of his initial plan.

"More like a Hail Mary," he scoffed. "This is my last chance. Otherwise, I'll be doomed until I eventually die." Adam immediately began jogging in place then doing push-ups, repeating the process over and over. After a few hours, Sevant slowly walked into Adam's cell.

With a calm yet victorious glow, Sevant grinned with a crooked smile.

"So, you enjoyed yesterday? Well, I sure did! It was a shame you only went two rounds, because I had so much more in the tank. Wouldn't have traded that moment for the world.

"Anyway, shithead, here are your rations for today. Unlike me, it looks like the doctor's taken a liking to you." Adam simply waited as Sevant revealed his tray of food.

Steamed sweetbread with a side of honey packets and a full stick of butter.

Next, baby carrots and broccoli served with a grilled chicken breast, and two glasses filled to the brim, one with water and one with milk. Finally, to top it off, a thick slice of chocolate cake.

"Hurry the hell up so I can clean this up, jerk off. Oh, and for your information, you punch like a girl." Adam ignored Sevant and utterly destroyed his meal, the flavors impacting upon his palate making him swoon. The colors of the food brilliantly shimmered against the bland white landscape as a peculiar sense of freedom rushed through Adam's mind.

The taste was superb, and this brief moment gave Adam a sense of humanity.

He wasn't just some monkey!

He could appreciate this meal, could understand what it took to survive and move forward.

And now, he found himself wondering if this was the voice's way of giving him a pat on the head. With that thought, Adam began to feel a surge of anger.

For a few moments, he felt as if he may have idolized the voice, and he was outraged at that thought. This was more akin to giving a lab rat a block of cheese for doing well.

Of course, he finished his meal but within the confines of his mind, he told himself that he owed nothing to the doctor, and his memory may have faded away but what little he did remember, he knew he was not here of his own free will.

He knew about the outside world and above all else, knew that the stem of all of his suffering emanated from this blasted doctor.

Funny, he thought. *It's almost as if I'm secretly seeking approval of anyone or anything. Trapped in a near colorless world devoid of compassion, hope, and peace.*

How much more could he take? And how much longer could he survive this? His mind kept slipping further and further into darkness. After his daily exercise routine, Adam could see the wall sliding and sure enough, quite predictable, Sevant's head poked out with a gleeful smile.

"Hey, cunt muffin. Time for the test to begin."

The test. The goddamned test…

Adam's eyes locked onto Sevant's, filled with a hatred like no other. Eyes piercing into his soul as if all along, he had been beneath him, looking at him the same way an outraged noble looks upon a peasant in disgust. Throughout his life, Sevant had never felt threatened by a patient. Typically, they would urinate themselves and begin to weep profusely at this point.

Until now, they would either fail a test or simply die by his hands. Yet this was the first time he had felt a sense of tension, and he knew that those eyes were a declaration of war.

Sevant simply returned his gaze with a more intense albeit barbaric glare.

"What's with the third-degree, shithead? You're going to get shocked three times today. You and I both know there is no way out of this. Unless, of course, you decide to off yourself, but then it may be a while before I get a new toy to play with."

Adam looked at Sevant calmly and his words came out clear, concise, and prophetic.

"Today is the day you die," Adam proclaimed. "Thinking things over, as I have little else to do… I didn't want to hurt you, and I sure as hell didn't want to kill you. But time and time again, you keep pushing me further and further off this cliff. Let's get this clear, you piece of shit.

"I'm done with being scared of you. I'm done with bowing and scraping to you. I'm not jumping and I'm not running anymore. Let's get this over with."

Sevant cautiously walked with Adam in silence, prepared for any tricks up the lab rat's sleeves. Nothing of harm or concern happened; they simply walked through the hall.

What was this uncertainty he felt?

He had been threatened before, but why did Adam's words run a cold sweat down his spine?

The only man on this earth Sevant had ever feared was the doctor himself. This bothered Sevant so much so, he decided to instigate this bug's train of thought.

"So, you're going to kill me? Is that it?" Sevant said plainly.

Adam remained silent as if savoring the moment.

"What, no rebuttal, cunt muffin? You can't just say you're going to kill someone and leave it at that. Haven't you learned any manners?" He slapped the back of Adam's head firmly, making sure that Adam knew the proper way of things.

He was weak while Sevant was strong.

Nothing more and nothing less; that was the way of things in the end.

"Access denied!" a robotic voice chirped as Adam pushed on one of the other cell block doors at random. Leaning in, Sevant spat on Adam's face.

"Don't you remember, dipshit? Nurses are the only ones with access, you dolt, and I don't even have the key card for this one."

Adam looked Sevant dead in the eyes and spat in *his* face.

"Fuck you!" Adam yelled, kicking Sevant right in the groin. A shocking wave of pain filled the brute. In response, however, Sevant retorted with a large, wide swing aimed at the young man's face. The giant fist smashing into Adam's face seemed a bit weaker than Sevant's normal strength. Still, as the momentum carried Sevant's arm, Adam clutched onto it like a feral cat clinging on for dear life. Sevant became unbalanced and it was at this precise moment that Adam bit down on Sevant's wrist while falling to the floor, bringing the mammoth down with him.

Once on the floor, Adam was taking more desperate fists to his face and torso, each hefty blow rattling his brain. Adam struggled and wrestled with Sevant—the sight akin to a small hare fighting desperately for its life against a ravenous boa constrictor. Even though it was a rather quick and clearly one-sided bout, both parties were breathing heavily. At some distance, any person might have mistaken it for a professional wrestling bout. Alas, it was not.

The strain on poor Adam was colossal now, setting him off coughing and sputtering as if his bloody guts and innards might make an appearance from his mouth anytime soon.

"You knew you'd lose, asshole!" Sevant stated with a wheeze. "Why would you even try? Kill me? I'll wager you don't even know the meaning of the word."

His eyes were still brimming with rage.

Adam lay on the ground beaten to a pulp, prostrate and in dead silence.

Sevant got up from the cold surface and clutched onto Adam, carrying him like a ragdoll and propping him up on his feet. "Let's go! C'mon, tough guy!" Sevant yelled out impatiently.

Adam's head was still reeling from their bout, and he could barely balance himself.

Each step he took felt sluggish and uncoordinated, his gait assuming the appearance of a man just fresh from a tavern after a full night's heavy drinking, veering this way and that, tripping over his own feet, lurching as though about to land again on his beaten face.

"Move ahead, dickhead!" Sevant screeched in utter frustration, pushing Adam forward forcefully. Yet this was more than Adam could have hoped for. Immediately after that initial push, Adam went hurtling at full speed through the hall, using every ounce of energy he had left.

"Fuck! Shit for brains, what are you doing?" Sevant yelled, chasing after Adam. "Come here, you piece of crap." Reaching the door several yards away from Sevant, Adam's goal had now been accomplished—to cause a ruckus and steal the key card from Sevant's pocket while he was enraged. Adam's face was swollen but the results had been well worth it.

Holding the key card close to the scanner caused its lights to flicker from red to green.

Adam twisted the handle and entered the testing area. Success.

After grabbing the pocketknife and opening a few boxes before the test had even begun, Adam could hear Sevant slamming against the door again and again, trying to break through it.

"Doc, let me the fuck in!" yelled Sevant in desperation behind the door, but the voice spoke out with clear resentment.

"Did I not give you a key card to enter in the first place? If you have misplaced it, feel free to grab yourself a spare at the main office," the doctor said.

"But that's down at the other end of the hall!" Sevant said in exasperation. "Come on, Doc. Let me in so I can beat this shit-for-brains prick!"

"Then I suggest you hurry. He's already opened about fifty percent of them, and I do not intend to start the timer until you have entered the room."

Sevant kicked the door in anger and sped off in the opposite direction.

With time finally on Adam's side and his plan appearing to have been something of a success, all that was left was a gamble. This was his last chance to get past the door.

He could feel Sevant's bloodlust boiling over, seeping through the small crevices of the cold metal door. In order to get closer to the doctor, he sensed that he needed to complete more tests.

With that in mind, there was more of a likelihood he would begin to understand the doctor better—this way, Adam could end this nightmare by also ending the life of the lunatic who had put him here. He would gain the doctor's confidence and kill him right there, where he stood.

Hopefully, he would then find a way out of this trash heap.

Everything was set. Adam had laid out four boxes in an unorganized fashion and the trick would be to make it seem that he was in the process of opening them with the pocketknife, and hopefully, Sevant wouldn't realize that he had the chance of finishing the test.

Adam grabbed the metal rod from the drawer and slid it underneath, out of sight.

All that remained now was to wait for Sevant to return, which wasn't going to take much longer as the lock audibly shifted with sounds of expletives behind it.

"Time begins now," the doctor's voice bellowed.

Sevant walked over to see Adam's progression.

It was far worse than he thought. Only four remained and the box with the note was still unopened. If Adam could figure out that all he needed to do was place the box outside the room, the jig was up. Not only would he pass the test, but it would also be because of his own doing.

The doctor would most definitely demote Sevant, that slimy weasel making him work his way back up to his current rank, going through the same process as he'd done many moons ago.

He prided himself as one of the top nurses in the facility, a nurse with his own room and all the luxuries he had ever wanted. Electronics, liquor, smokes, and even on occasion, women.

Scarce were the days that he remembered once being a patient at this facility himself, struggling to survive just like Adam. However, it had been easier before; the doctor had actually been lenient then and had made several mistakes. Sevant was lucky to have survived and become a nurse during those times. Now, it was nothing like that anymore; it was almost hopeless.

This place was simply a slaughterhouse and year after year came more and more failures that no one had ever heard about. The tests were now so difficult that it must have been at least eleven years or so since any patient had actually become a nurse that way.

They typically either died or killed themselves.

He'd be damned if he'd let this irregular patient succeed even in one test.

Sevant would probably lose nearly everything considering how abrasive he had been with the doctor. He was lost in thought for a few moments, feeling uncertainty and a tinge of regret.

Shortly after, Sevant noticed that Adam seemed to have become more cautious of the note. Not only that, but he hadn't even opened a single box since he'd come in.

What was his aim? It didn't matter, as long as he didn't carry the box with the note outside the door. Hell, as long as there were just two boxes opened and the rest thrown out the door, Adam would pass, making things oh so difficult for Sevant.

Adam no longer had the shadow of fear in his eyes, which perplexed Sevant.

Rather than regressing and becoming a shell of a human being, even after every beating and shock therapy, Adam still pressed on.

In secret, Sevant was impressed by Adam's efforts and resilience.

Adam was showing promise even if it meant at his own expense.

Sevant debated whether or not to beat him to a pulp after the test was over—a show of respect from one past patient to another. At least the thought made Sevant chuckle.

"No, he's going to get his ass whooped severely for what he pulled," Sevant said. Time was almost up so in routine, Sevant searched the drawer for the metal rod.

"What the hell!" he screamed out in agony as blood flowed along his right arm. "You've gone too far this time, you have. You're going to pay for this."

Adam had jammed the pocketknife firmly into Sevant's arm. The pain was sharp and prickly, yet he'd had far worse than this. It was a mere flesh wound by comparison to what had passed before. What angered Sevant most was not the pain, but the sheer audacity of this patient.

In utter outrage, he retaliated swiftly, pushing Adam to the floor with all his might, knocking the wind right out of him.

"Are you that serious about pissing me the fuck off?" Sevant screamed.

This is it, Adam thought, *the moment I've been waiting for.*

And yes, he really was that serious about pissing off Sevant. It was going down a treat so far!

Adam had opened two boxes, leaving only the one box with the note and an extra. With Sevant's back turned, he set about searching frantically for the rod, readying himself to find that thing and put it to use.

Really? Pissing you right off, am I?

And it looks like I'm doing a good job of it!

He searched around even more. Where was that goddamn rod?

Under here, you jackass… Surely, it's under here.

But still, the rod did not surface.

Ah, but there was still the blade. But the blade was where, now…?

Damn thing's still embedded in that dirty bastard's arm…

He lurched forward, quicker than the eye could see, yanking the small pocketknife blade from Sevant's bloodied arm and suddenly, Sevant felt an incredible surge of pain.

A flash of cold metal greeted the air, and now Sevant was getting the full force of the small steel blade piercing his neck!

Again, in a heartbeat, Adam withdrew it quickly, now stabbing the knife deep into Sevant's left arm. The movements from one to the other left him no time to think, let alone breathe.

But he could scream. There was always screaming…

"Fuck!" Sevant's agonized shriek assaulted the air between them, sending it up into the eaves. Turning around without hesitation, Sevant swung with all his might in Adam's direction, but his fist collided against a box Adam was holding up against his own chest. Sevant's eyes widened and there was no time for his brain to react and put on the brakes.

The box popped open with the tape mangled, a small crack appearing.

It still was open, nonetheless. Bleeding heavily and filled with adrenaline, Sevant chased Adam down, ready to drive his fist onto Adam's feeble skull.

Adam grabbed the last box on the floor and opened it.

Holding the knife desperately to his chest, he curled into the fetal position.

Adam accepted the blows like a punching bag of flesh.

Sevant, still angry, yelled at the top of his lungs, "If you think this changes anything, you're wrong, dickhead!"

"Time is up," the doctor announced through another speaker.

Sevant continued kicking and beating Adam, then set about strangling him. The blood from both Sevant's arm and neck cascaded all down Adam's face, covering it in blood, his hands desperately clawing at the giant hands strapped around his neck.

Adam could feel his consciousness slipping.

"Enough! The test has ended," the doctor's voice said.

It was stern, almost as if he was angry. "Now then, *this* was unexpected," said the doctor. "Give me a few moments to analyze what has transpired."

Sevant panted, waiting for the doctor's orders. Waiting for Adam's inevitable death.

He may have posed a threat before. However, attacking a nurse, now that was a clear violation not only against Sevant, but by extension, it was a challenge to the doctor's authority.

The box may have stated, 'whoever opens this box will die', but the doctor wouldn't just let the patient do as they pleased.

Sevant wanted to tear Adam apart, but the blood loss was too great, and he could feel the sluggish sensation coursing through his body. He also didn't want to anger the doctor any further. Instead, he simply administered first aid on himself using materials from within the drawer.

***

Elsewhere, in a dim-lit room, a ragged old man in a lab coat clenched the hairs on his head, laughing hysterically. "I didn't see this outcome at all! What an interesting subject! All the boxes have been opened!" And yet, the old man couldn't finish his sentence as he broke into laughter even more. The doctor's voice returned at a more audible volume.

"Adam, you have passed the test. Please proceed to the next door."

"What!" Sevant yelled. "Don't you get it, halfwit? He broke the rules!"

Without hesitation, Adam quickly opened the door and pressed on, able to feel that today would be the last one on which he'd ever have to deal with Sevant again.

Sevant slammed against the door, calling out to Adam in a frenzy, "You asshole, you think this is over. I'll fucking kill you! I'll kill you nice and slow!"

Adam smirked at Sevant's idle threats.

All he had to do now was await the doctor's orders.

He'd taken a gamble and he'd succeeded, the grim reaper's scythe dangling above his head at any moment. Rather than cower, Adam decided to play with the reaper, for in the end, whether he obeyed or risked it all, he was a dead man anyway. Though trying as best he could, he still couldn't ignore Sevant's pathetic cries emanating from the other side of the door.

The doctor's voice echoed through the room in a menacing chuckle.

"I'm sorry, Sevant. My hands are tied. I didn't explicitly say he couldn't start the test early." Sevant could see that wide evil grin the doctor had. He didn't need to be in the room to know when the doctor was lusting after the death of a patient or rather in this case, a nurse.

"Please, Doc. I didn't mean the things I said. Just don't do this, please!" Sevant begged.

"But Sevant, think about it from my side. You let a patient steal the key card, and you expected me to allow you to enter? And worst of all, you had the guile to demand it!"

The doctor's voice became stern and cold.

"You have the audacity to beg mercy from me, have you? You opened the box, you fool. How do you think it would make me look if I allowed you to live? I'm a man of my word, after all." Sevant's eyes widened, tears streaming down his face as he heard the doctor's horrible news. "You opened the box, Sevant. My hands are tied, you see."

Attempting to hold back laughter, the doctor clasped his mouth with his hand but not before giving off a slight chuckle. Sevant continued to weep and wail with cries of anguish.

It was at this spectacle that the doctor could no longer keep his composure. This gorilla of a man prided himself in his strength and his false sense of machismo. To see his persona peeled off and reduced to this state was simply too amusing. The doctor began laughing through the intercom uncontrollably, hacking and coughing, attempting to form words.

"You buffoon. He played you like a harp!"

More snickering and laughter ensued.

Sevant ran toward the end of the room, banging against the door over and over, flailing about and trying to open the door—but it was all to no avail.

The doctor had locked it as soon as Adam entered.

"Please, sir. I don't want to die. Please, I don't want to die!" Sevant shouted, his tears merging into a torrential stream as his mouth quivered.

Words became guttural noises as Sevant couldn't contain all the emotions bellowing out of his mind. He held his head in dismay and disbelief.

"Please have mercy on me. I'll learn, I promise. I won't step out of line ever again! Please!"

The doctor's voice became stern again. "You know how this works. You were a fan of this when it was dealt out to the others, remember? So, allow me to impart some wisdom before your brain shuts down all bodily functions along with it."

Chapter 4

Sevant pleaded, begging over the doctor's words in cries for redemption and mercy.

In the grand scheme of things, life is merely an illusion and your life as well as mine is meaningless. Dead silence permeated the room, Sevant lying on the floor, staring at the ceiling.

He could feel the toxin releasing from within his right shoulder, numbness proceeding from the ends of his extremities as he called out to Adam.

"Help me! Adam, help me! Please," Sevant said, tears running down his face. "I'm sorry for calling you names and beating you to a pulp! It was all in good fun, wasn't it? Just please come here and give me a hand, won't you? Adam! Can you hear me? Adam, please! I'm sorry. I'm so sorry," Sevant stated in a whimpering tone.

Adam heard his pleas and could no longer stand idly by.

He walked toward the door and noticed that from his side, he could open it if he so chose.

Adam twisted the handle firmly and walked over to Sevant, finding him stunned.

Even after all the humiliation and despair Sevant had caused him, after all his torment, Adam was actually willing to help him! "What do you need me to do?" Adam asked reluctantly.

"There is this capsule releasing poison into my right shoulder. Use your knife and cut it out of me, please!" Adam carefully inserted the knife in the general direction as Sevant traced the path over his shoulder with his left hand. Adam could feel a decent-sized object hitting against the tip of the blade. It must still have been tucked underneath a few centimeters of flesh.

The pain was excruciating, and Sevant nearly bit through his tongue as the agony reverberated within his shoulder, a sign that the adrenaline must have been beginning to wear off.

"There," Adam said as he pulled out a capsule size of a peaches pit.

"Thank you! Oh God, thank you!" Sevant stated in pure gratitude.

As the tears kept flowing through Sevant's eyes, Adam simply responded with a nod.

Sevant was a broken man now, all his pride stripped away.

All his grandeur and male bravado were merely an illusion he had created, all to cover up a scared man barely clinging onto his frail sanity. His left arm was losing all functionality and his neck had stopped bleeding, but he could barely shift his head for fear of reopening the wound.

His shoulder ached. Adam ripped off the lower half of his shirt using the knife, wrapping it tightly over the incision he had created.

"Now, I need you to take this key card and run to the other end of the hall," Sevant said in distress. "The doctor will need forty-five minutes at the most before he can change the access codes. From there, head to the infirmary. You can't miss it; there are signs and room numbers past the hall of your cell block. Come back here with two first aid kits and as many sharp medical tools as you can find. Believe it or not, this whole facility doesn't have any firearms.

"The only exception to that is the doctor carrying a Berretta." After receiving the key card, Adam stayed silent and motionless. "Hurry! He's probably already sending someone to finish the job!" Sevant said. "If you grab what we need, we can make a stand here and now!"

"I doubt that's going to be necessary," Adam replied coldly, slowly walking toward the empty drawers and gabbing the electric rod underneath. Sevant's eyes widened as he realized in sheer horror that there was no longer any hope for salvation.

"Please, dear God. No, don't do this! I'm sorry! Please, you have to understand I was like you once! I'm not well in the head! This place is what made me like this! It tore at my very soul, and I couldn't take it anymore! So, I decided to like it, to like the chaos and accept it as a part of me! I know that was a mistake. I know I hurt hundreds of patients but please, don't let the cycle continue! You and I can put a stop to this madness if we work together! Please don't kill me!"

Adam drove his foot with all his might and strength across Sevant's face while he lay barren on the ground. He then continued his violent assault with several kicks to the face and groin.

Adam's relentless barrage of abuse made his breath uneven and raspy, and he continued to beat this man until exhaustion overcame him. His knuckles were a bloodied and sweaty mess, and his feet ached from the constant contact against Sevant's ribs.

By the end of it all, Sevant's face was akin to a smashed grapefruit, or a tenderized steak. His nose had been bent and several teeth were missing, his lips a bloodied pulpy mess.

Adam even took the liberty of breaking the man's limbs, grabbing each one in turn and using all his weight to snap them like twigs.

Adam then took the electric rod and pushed it against Sevant's right eye. The screams of this man turned into a melody when they reached Adam's ears. "Here, why not have a taste? What's the saying again? Seconds out, round three," Adam said calmly.

The shock surged throughout Sevant's body. He convulsed continually, shaking and screaming out his string of obscenities. "Fuck you!" he yelled out in defiance.

Adam just held onto the trigger, studying Sevant's face quietly.

Sevant's right eye set off smoking as the constant shock cooked it from the inside out, caving in the eyeball, blackening the color of the whole. With each press of the trigger, Sevant seized and convulsed into what looked like poses. *It's almost like interpretive dance,* Adam thought as a small smirk of joy formed across his face. When he'd had his fill, Adam grabbed the knife from his pocket and knelt down before the now faceless Sevant. He glared at Sevant's one good eye.

"Didn't I tell you, asshole, you're dying today! Didn't you believe me?" Adam yelled with overflowing rage as he plunged the steel into Sevant's flesh. Over and over, the blade tore into Sevant as the blood gushed forth all over Adam's hands and Sevant's torso, his screams echoing through the room. Begging and pleading for Adam to relent, he urinated on himself.

His agony became unbearable, his loss all too great for his weak-willed mind to handle.

With smashed lips and missing teeth, he gurgled his last words in a barely audible tone.

"I don't want to die… I don't…" The words slurred and jumbled, and blood began sliding out through the open crevices of his mouth. "Help… me… I'm so cold."

Dead silence fell across the room. All that remained was a mush of a corpse, mangled and smashed, bright red blood spattered across the white walls and pools of blood slowly spreading across the floor. Sevant, the tall and powerful alpha male, died as a helpless child in fear.

Adam felt as though he'd regained some of his dignity after all he had been through.

He spat on what he assumed to be Sevant's butchered face and moved to the next room, knowing he would have been caught fairly easily if he'd tried going to the infirmary.

Sevant was wishing the impossible.

There was a reason for this place still being in operation. If it were that easy, he wouldn't be a prisoner here now, would he? Adam was not planning on simply attempting an escape; he wanted assurance, something concrete, a way of getting out and never coming back to this place.

The doctor spoke, accompanied by a clapping of hands. "Congratulations, Adam. What a show! Now, the other way of passing the test was to simply move the box of death outside of the testing area." The doctor chuckled. "However unorthodox that was, you still achieved your goal, so it's still a success. Now then, you have permission to speak and ask questions. However, I am not inclined to answer them if I feel no need to. So, fire away, but Adam, please be sensible."

Adam had hundreds of questions to hurl at the doctor, but he knew most of them wouldn't aid in his survival. Thinking carefully, Adam responded.

"I have a few you can answer after I have asked my fill," said Adam. The presumptuous nature elated the doctor. Not knowing his place tantalized him somewhat.

"Go on," the doctor said playfully.

"Had I tried killing Sevant directly, would I have been killed? And if I had attempted to help Sevant, would I have been successful? And also, will you be assigning me a new nurse?"

The doctor pondered for a moment, considering whether or not to divulge.

Looking at Adam through a screen in a dim lit room, he answered, "I don't *believe* I would have killed you. I would have been annoyed mostly and then replaced Sevant with someone more... someone more flexible. However, having said that, if you were to become too problematic, you'd force my hand." He showed empathy.

"Have no fear, Adam. Simply partake in more tests with the goal to solve them. The more tests you pass, the more privileges you will have."

Adam could see where this was going.

Even if he continued passing more tests and attaining certain privileges, the doctor was still in control; he'd tried killing Sevant with poison without any hesitation even after years of service to him. People were easily dispensable to him and gaining the doctor's trust seemed long out of reach. But if Adam saw an opportunity, then he would certainly take his chance.

"Now, as for attempting an escape or a rescue of some sort, well that would have been proven useless. Sevant would have died even with your intervention. That toxin within his body is so potent, and just a few ounces can kill a full-grown man in a matter of minutes.

"The amount each capsule holds should have killed him in less than ten minutes give or take. In the end, however, you seemed to prefer having him die a much quicker yet more painful death." The doctor chuckled. "Fools like you have no understanding."

The doctor spoke in pity. "However, I am willing to teach you, Adam. Anger, sadness, and happiness are all meaningless. Life itself is meaningless. However, with these tests and ordeals that you will go through, they will give your life a purpose.

"The purpose of creating meaning in a meaningless existence."

Adam couldn't understand, nor did he want to. As far as he was concerned, this doctor was mentally unstable and had a sick and twisted sense of humor, devoid of any empathy or mercy.

The doctor's voice became stern and rigid.

"Adam, you will never leave this place even when you have fulfilled your purpose as a patient. You will always have to work for me until the day you breathe your last breath."

Adam's fists clenched, his teeth gritting together, and his anger boiling over inside of him.

He desperately tried to hold his tongue, knowing he needed to bide his time.

The doctor was bound to slip up at some point and when that time came, Adam would be there to end this unhinged man's life. Adam had created his own solution and his own fate today.

Neither Sevant nor the doctor expected things to end that way.

With that point in mind, Adam tuned out the doctor's voice and searched the room as the doctor explained his new nurse would soon like to meet him within the next room.

The room was just a solid shade of white like his previous cell except this time, there wasn't a cage, just a small white couch and a white fridge. Adam sat down, took a breath, and opened the fridge. To the side of the door, cans of sodas and other refreshments were in abundance, and he grabbed several bottles of water and the most familiar drink he could find.

Cracking open the can made a hissing sound so very familiar.

With that, as Adam drank the sweet effervescent liquid, he recalled his days in early childhood, running around the playground playing tag as an elderly woman handed out drinks for the kids. A single tear ran down Adam's face as the sense of nostalgia dug deep into his heart.

Tasting this drink calmed him, making him feel human again. The room was about the same size of the cage but there were no bars and a sense of freedom reigned within the colorless space. Also, there was the white couch several times more comfortable than the worn, thin yet bumpy mattress. There was even a small portable toilet he could use.

Everything else was just as plain as the last room in which he'd been sleeping.

Just as the doctor was finishing his explanation about his imminent provision of the nurse, Adam found what he suspected the doctor was looking through.

It was barely visible in one corner of the room.

Attached to the ceiling was an incredibly small camera, camouflaged by also being white. The lens itself could not have been more than the size of a penny.

Staring into the camera directly, Adam's eyes were sharp and full of determination.

So, this was how the spying went on.

The doctor paused for a moment and grinned staring back into Adam's eyes.

"It's because of people like you that I come to realize how much I enjoy my work, Adam."

"What's the next test then, Doctor?" Adam replied, ignoring the doctor's previous statement. There was no point in responding to something like that, feeding the man's facetious comments.

"Take a load off, Adam. Tomorrow is a big day, so don't

disappoint me."

The doctor got up from his chair and left the room, shutting off the light.

Once again, Adam was back to being by himself, alone with his thoughts. Flopping onto the couch, Adam calmed himself and rested his head. Tomorrow might be a big day but for now, Adam could rest and hopefully dream of a far better place than this.

***

The day-to-day scenarios of humans are incredibly mundane, I do find.

To consume, rest, and procreate, that is all it comes down to, forming social connections or hobbies to fill in the blanks of the remainder of time humans have on this earth. What profit is there when man decides to distract himself and ignore his overall impending doom?

Life is so swift, you see, and even if everything is happenstance with nothing fated to be, it would be nice to observe and study longer, don't you think?

Human instinct clings to life so desperately, and the questions I ask myself seem only to breed more questions, and so it goes on, a perpetual study in which the results lead only to more tests, more aspects to consider and research. Life itself has been a mistake.

Yet now that man has already spilt the milk, what now can he do to break its cycle, to push the barriers by which he has found himself constrained for thousands of years?

What can we learn from man's struggle for survival? What can we learn from the breaking point of the mind? Therein lies the key to true meaning.

Not a fabrication, not a distraction, and not the ingrained instinct of mere monkey.

The path forward will be long and difficult. Yet I will rise above it all, gifting to mankind our true purpose wrapped in pretty bows of bloody violence.

***

Adam's body felt the weight and struggles of the day before, his muscles sending signals of distress and discomfort. His head was feeling as if he must had placed it in an oven and his eyes had fallen prey to a stinging sensation. He rose from the couch, yawning and blinking.

Quickly, his senses sharpened as he jumped up off the couch again, yelping like a flustered mutt. A short yet stocky man with scars all over his face was standing before him.

"God, you almost gave me a heart attack. How long have you been standing there?"

"About thirty minutes, give or take. The name is Atreus," the odd man said.

Adam just stood there perplexed, waiting for a beating since it seemed unlikely the man had made an appearance for any other purpose.

"Why are you looking at me like that? It's actually very uncomfortable," Atreus said.

"Let's just say you're a bit different than my last nurse," Adam replied.

"Yeah, seems likes you two had some little disagreements, that's for sure. I could hardly miss it, could I? All that blood is crusty and dry now, by the way, but you might like to take a look at yourself because it's all over your clothes. You smell like garbage and your hair is all matted."

Not often taking into account his own appearance, Adam realized how mangled and disturbed he must have looked to others. Dried blood covered the floor, and the couch bore a large and unpleasant stain via a splash of bright red.

His clothes were also still slightly moist from Sevant's congealed blood.

Atreus quickly walked over to a cart he'd brought in with him.

"First, give me your clothes so I can throw them out and wash you up."

Adam complied and even though Sevant had done the very same thing, it was odd for yet another man to wash him and clean off the grime from his flesh.

"Here, put these on. Oh, and don't think I don't know you have that pocketknife up your ass. So, give it up," Atreus said with authority, his hand outstretched, expecting Adam to relinquish the blade. With great reluctance, Adam handed the knife over.

Everything appeared to be normal except for the shirt.

A strange ornate symbol had been stitched into the fabric near his left breast, a small circle with two triangles in its center. Both triangles were facing opposite ends, connected on top of one another to create a diamond shape. "What's this, Atreus?" asked Adam, pointing to the symbol.

Atreus stood there in silence for a time, staring blankly at the symbol as if Adam had not spoken a word. Confused, Adam rose his hand instinctively, sticking it up high in the air.

He looked like a child in a daycare.

"Listen, I really don't care for those proper manners the doctor is so fond of," voiced Atreus at last. "As we both know, I'm stuck here, and you're stuck here. Least we can do is relax when we can," Atreus said with a sigh. "Was lost in thought is all. That's the doctor's emblem.

"Look at it again and you'll see it's a diamond made of two triangles encased in a circle. I have no idea what it means. The doctor is cryptic as always. Go figure. Am I right?"

Atreus' voice had a gleeful tone. Adam was a bit caught off guard by his carefree attitude, almost as if it was alien to him. He remembered faintly what it was like to socialize for the sake of socializing but yet again, there was still such a haze in his memories.

He couldn't quite piece anything together; he simply 'knew' things.

Atreus picked up a mop and started to clean the room's floors.

"Food is over there. Just sit on the floor till I'm done with the couch. You really gave me a chore today, sheesh." Adam couldn't tell if this was some kind of act or maybe that Atreus could be slightly unhinged in other areas. It almost appeared as if he was relishing the mopping task, as if it made him feel useful or important. *To be honest,* Adam thought, *besides the mangled scars and burns all over his face, he appears to be quite a decent fellow.*

Clean-cut hair, a modest build of muscle and a welcoming voice. A tolerable demeanor too!

A man could do worse than have Atreus to keep him company in a cell.

He felt too normal, in fact, as if he belonged somewhere so very far away from this place.

Adam looked at the food, a small loaf of bread with half a stick of butter and a cup of baked beans. On the side of the plate were small packets of jelly and a glass of milk.

Adam grabbed his tray full of food in delight and sat on the floor, pulling apart the bread and drowning its pieces in jelly. He took a few swigs of the beans until they were no more.

Adam then ate the butter whole while tearing at the sticky bread he had created.

Having consumed all the food, he chugged the milk down in seconds. All the while, Atreus stood there staring at Adam.

"You're a bit of a pig, aren't you?" he said.

"I was starving. Not that I'd expect a nurse to understand how it feels. So, I'm sorry.

"I guess waking up in the middle of nowhere and being tortured constantly makes you forget about table manners. My sincere apology if it offends you."

Atreus frowned and gave Adam a pitiful glare after his short speech.

"You think you're the only one here with problems? Let's get one thing straight. I'm not a sadist like Sevant was, but I can see why he was. All of us nurses were once patients like you.

"You either adapt or die. You can whine and complain all you like, but how far will that get you? All that matters is to stay alive and try to learn how to be happy with what you have.

"As for Sevant, he enjoyed giving patients hell. Yeah, he was an asshole, but this place turned him into who he was. Sanity in this place is a rare commodity. Soon, you'll lose yours too."

Adam was taken aback, feeling a tinge of regret from his last retort.

He understood Atreus, grasping that he was simply giving him advice. And he had to admit, he did need advice to help him bear the weight of this place.

He looked at his new nurse in disbelief. "If what you're saying is true, then why are you being so nice to me? Why do you seem perfectly normal?"

Atreus sighed and gathered his cleaning tools back to his cart.

"Look, Adam. I'm not at liberty to say anything about what tests you'll be undergoing, but I *can* tell you what I've dealt with and by the end of it, you'll realize I'm not what you would call nice at all. I value my life more than anyone else's. And take it from me, I'd strangle you to death if that's what the doctor wanted. I'm here to do my job."

Adam knew it to be true. Atreus wasn't much of a coward, but he was honest enough to admit his fear of death. Adam looked into his eyes and could almost feel the weight they carried.

They were eyes that must have seen unimaginable horrors…

So much so that they were dull and devoid of any glimmer to them.

"So, what tests have you undergone then, Atreus?" he asked with curiosity.

Again, the man was refreshing, Atreus proving to be very open and frank, explaining.

"Besides his typical puzzles, the doctor has had me kill a couple dozen or so people, those I've never met. He has had me eat the flesh of the dead and even of the living.

"Hell, I've even had to dismember myself."

Atreus lifted his pant leg, revealing a prosthetic limb. He tapped on it in a joking manner.

Then he continued, "These burns and scars are from penalties and the doctor's twisted sense of humor." Adam's jaw dropped and he was sweating. "Listen well, Adam. What you've gone through so far was unpleasant, I'll give you that, but it was child's play.

"You need to be prepared for anything and expect only the worst. If you can survive long enough, then you can become a nurse and from there, you'll have your own room and anything you desire within reason. All you'll have to do is clean up after the doctor's patients until the day you die. Frankly, it's only a few hours in a day, so really it could be someone's dream job."

Atreus gave a mild chuckle.

Adam fell silent for a time, unsure if he had the mental fortitude to cut off his own finger let alone a whole leg.

The thought of cannibalism made his stomach retch too.

His hands still had a slight tremble after brutally killing his tormentor, and he could only imagine the toll on his heart if it'd been someone who hadn't done a thing to him.

"Is he really that crazy?" Adam said in disdain and Atreus nodded his head.

"Oh, he's way worse than that. I have only spoken of the best bits, his mildest attributes. The doctor is probably the worst one of all. I woke up the same as you, not knowing who I was or where I came from and after thirty years, I've just begun piecing together my life before this.

"He does this for fun you know. He claims that all this furthers his research, but I can't see the rhyme or reason to it." Atreus looked up at the ceiling. "I have been longing to see the blue sky and feel the sun's warmth. I have slight glimpses of how it felt so long ago, but no more than that." Atreus looked back at Adam.

"You're already going to live in this hell. What's the point in tearing at your sanity? This place will do just that alone. That's why Sevant died. He kept poking the bear, didn't he?"

Clenching his fists, Adam looked down at his feet.

"Well, he got what was coming to him, Sevant did. Sevant was a disgusting prick who kept beating me senseless! I'm glad I killed him!" Adam yelled in rage.

Atreus walked over to Adam, patting him hard on his back.

"You don't have to justify anything to me, kid."

Atreus walked away with the cart, exiting the room. "Oh, next test is going to be tomorrow. Might want to rest up and try to relax for today. See you tomorrow."

As Atreus left, Adam felt perplexed. He was in a better room and had a better nurse, yet he couldn't help but have a horrible premonition of what was to come next.

He lay back down on his freshly cleaned couch and drifted into a deep sleep.

Chapter 5

"Wake up, Adam!" the doctor yelled through the speaker. Adam startled at the rather loud and abrupt noise, jumping upright from the couch. "Time to test. Aren't you excited, Adam?"

The doctor's voice was playful.

"If you can pass this, then you'll have more amenities at your disposal. Exercising every day is all well and good, but what about your downtime? I'm sure staring at the ceiling for hours on end is still boring, don't you think?"

"So, where is Atreus?" Adam replied.

"He is at the testing area. You're allowed to proceed through the next door."

Sure enough, Adam opened the door and there was Atreus waiting patiently. Within the room were a table and a chair, blending in with the stark white aesthetic. On the table itself were lying four clear glasses, a white jug with a sealed top, a black cloth, and a small syringe.

Adam prepared himself, standing tall and prepared for the worst just as Atreus had advised. The doctor's teeth reflected off of the screen's glow as his smirk formed into a smile.

"You must fill each of these glasses to the brim with liquid. When the time begins, Atreus will blindfold you. Within the jug is pure water. By the end of the test, the jug should be completely empty. The syringe is nothing more than a tool, you see, so use it how you see fit.

"You must not allow the floors to contact any liquid whatsoever. Finally, the time limit is fifteen minutes. Oh, and one simple rule: no solids within the glasses. In other words, no vomiting of any kind. Fail this test, and you will receive a penalty and as before, should you fail the first time *and* the next, then the penalties will begin to stack up further."

Adam's heart pounded, his senses sharpening, and the hairs on the back of his neck rising.

"Atreus will remove a finger of your choosing for each failed attempt."

The adrenaline spiked within Adam's body as he knew he couldn't afford to fail once, otherwise tremendous pain and loss would be the price.

"Your time begins… now," said the doctor.

Immediately, Atreus rushed to Adam's side, wrapping the blindfold across his eyes. Atreus clearly didn't want to harm Adam; however, they both knew that he would do anything if it meant his own survival. Adam was in front of the table searching with his hands ahead of him.

He could feel the glasses on the table, and as he reached even further, he could feel the handle of the jug. Grasping it firmly, Adam ripped the seal off, grabbed a glass and filled it with water.

He filled the first glass and the next, dragging his fingers across the edges of the glass to make sure they were both full to the brim. He had filled two of the three now.

Worryingly, Adam could feel the weight of the jug. It was empty, devoid of any substance.

"He wants my blood," Adam said, hoping Atreus would give him alternatives.

"Looks like it," Atreus said softly. "But are you sure that's the only liquid your body has to offer?" Atreus said with a softhearted chuckle.

"Atreus!" the doctor's voice screeched through the intercom. "You are to oversee the experiment, not provide assistance!"

"I apologize, Doctor. However, I don't believe that constitutes as assistance. I merely asked him a question." The doctor's face cringed and contorted as the sheen of light from the glowing screen traversed his old, weathered face.

"Then remain silent. Are we clear?"

"Yes, Doctor, understood," Atreus said with a smirk and Adam smiled.

Atreus was actually on his side. He might even think of him as a friend. Immediately, Adam removed his pants and undergarments. Grabbing the third glass, he imagined himself urinating.

Careful to avoid any spillage, he gently grasped his nether regions and shot out short bursts of warm urine into the glass. He felt slightly embarrassed, but this solution had to be better than having his fingers removed. He tried his best, but could only fill the glass a quarter of the way.

Nervously, Adam began searching for the syringe, rubbing his hands across the table.

It was do or die as far as he was concerned. Grasping the syringe, a cold chill ran down Adam's spine. His intuition screamed into his subconscious that this test was too easy.

Why have they blindfolded me? he thought. *What's the purpose? What if the syringe itself is somehow tainted?* He had never injected a syringe into a vein before.

What if the amount of blood he needed would kill him?

What if, by digging away into his flesh with a syringe in a place he couldn't see, he hit an artery and bled out? His thoughts were leading him to a place he didn't wish to go, spiraling out of control, theory after theory stacking one upon another. Adam's throat clenched, swelling up.

"Ten minutes left, Adam," the doctor said through the intercom.

Adam's mind wavered, and whether it was purely out of desperation or acute instincts, Adam stripped the blindfold away from his face. No warning and no signs of the test being over.

Besides, the doctor never said he could not take off the blindfold in the first place. Looking at the contents of the table, Adam had nearly finished with this test, and he began inspecting the syringe itself. The tip was not hollow, nor did it have a component to withdraw any blood.

The more he inspected it, the more he realized it was a very sharp prop. The minute he even tried extracting his blood it would leak all over the floor and the test would be a failure.

It was a well disguised shiv, so to speak.

"What is this thing?" Adam spoke aloud, looking at Atreus. Without saying a word, Atreus shifted his eyes toward Adam's feet. It was only a second, but Adam caught the gesture.

Adam quickly began searching the ground beneath his feet, yet there was nothing but a pure white laminated floor. Right then, it hit him. Adam rummaged about underneath the table.

The table itself did not possess four legs but a very thick pillar and upon closer inspection, it appeared to have gaps within itself. Right into the pillar was a small hole no larger than the tip of the oddly shaped shiv. Adam pressed the sharp pointed end into the tiny hole.

A square-shaped hatch swung open. Within it lay a small jug sitting inside of the hollowed-out pillar. "Five minutes remaining," the doctor's voice said with clear hints of frustration.

Adam placed the jug onto the table. However, there was a bit of a snag; he found the cap molded onto the jug, and no matter how much he twisted, it would not come off. Again, Adam resorted to using the shiv, poking holes onto the tip of the cap and from there, pouring its contents. Everything worked smoothly, filling the last glass with two minutes to spare.

"You have passed this test. Please proceed to the next room ahead of you," the doctor said in a seemingly foul mood. Adam walked toward the door and looked directly at Atreus's eyes.

"Thank you," Adam said. In return, Atreus smiled softly.

The next room was just as blank as the last, white walls all around from the floor to the ceiling. However, this time it came with a full-sized fridge, a comfortable looking bed, an exposed toilet, and a shower.

"So, it appears even with my warnings, your new nurse seems to be rather intrigued with you, Adam. Of course, he has always been quite the pushover. Yet never forget, he may not bear his fangs like Sevant did repeatedly, but upon my orders he will kill you without any hesitation," said the doctor, emphasizing to Adam not to get too complacent.

Adam's teeth were grinding as he heard the doctor's voice slither out through the intercom.

"I know that very well. So, what's the next test, then?" he asked in anger.

"Oh, aren't we the eager beaver!" The doctor laughed. "You should know by now it is just one test per day. Enjoy your new humble abode. I'm sure you'll be needing a nice rest."

The doctor's voice stung to the very core of Adam's heart.

How long am I going to be stuck like this?

'A nice rest' indeed!

His thoughts were running wildly, making him feel as if he was climbing an incredibly steep cliff. Just one slip-up and it was certain death. His mind felt as if a thousand knives were digging slowly into his skull. Passing that test for the first time had been a Godsend.

Adam gripped his left hand, imagining what it would be like had he failed the test.

What would have happened if someone other than Atreus had been his nurse? Someone just as sadistic and bloodthirsty as Sevant? He shuddered at the thought.

After collecting himself, Adam walked over to the exposed shower. Little privacy.

Just a drain, a faucet, and a shower head.

Tossing his clothes aside, he stared directly at the shower head then closed his eyes, slowly turning the handle. Warm water bathed his face, cascading across his torso.

Not once had he ever had the chance to clean himself. It felt like heaven itself.

Ever since he'd woken up strapped to that thin rickety mat, he had always had someone else wash him off. It was degrading and now, he started to feel more dignified and independent.

Pushing his head against the wall as the water kept flowing, Adam simply inhaled and exhaled, thinking that ever since his experiences with Sevant, he'd become numb to fear. Yet the doctor always had something up his sleeve to race his adrenaline and anxiety.

"No soap, huh?" Atreus said aloud. Adam flinched and tried to compose himself.

"Didn't know you were in here," Adam replied.

"I wasn't, bonehead. I just got in here. Liking the shower, are we?" Atreus wore a sheepish grin.

"Well, I would if I actually had some privacy." Adam refused to turn his head to meet Atreus's eye level given his current nakedness.

"Catch," Atreus said and Adam scuffled about, looking for the thrown object. Turned out it was a bar of soap. Adam's reaction time was slow, and it bumped him on his forehead.

"Gee, thanks," Adam replied with clear annoyance.

As he began lathering himself, Atreus spoke with a somber tone.

"Listen, what I did back there, don't expect that ever again. Doctor's orders. He pulled me to his office today after I cleaned the test area."

Adam shut the water off and finally looked at Atreus.

Adam's mouth dropped and his eyes widened.

"Oh shit! What the fuck happened in there?" Adam yelled.

Atreus smirked. "What always happens if I try and interfere with his tests." Atreus's eyes were both swollen, and his left arm was covered in a gauze drenched in his blood. His feet were bandaged with yet again, soaked in even more of his blood.

"He just threatened to demote me."

Atreus looked at Adam's horrified face and started explaining.

"No worries, this happens about twice a year," Atreus stated while pointing at himself with his right thumb. "I think I'm really more of just a torture doll for his frustration."

He spoke his opinions in a meek tone as if talking of the weather or of something inconsequential. "I've done a lot worse, really. I once tried aiding an escape and of course, we failed. He killed all the nurses who'd tried to escape except for me and Sevant.

"He didn't kill the two of us just because he had something better in mind. He had us helplessly watch as he dissected them alive, ripping out organ after organ, but he actually didn't beat me that time. Guess it was more a case of psychological torture. Wouldn't you agree?"

"So, he tortured you today even though you didn't really break any rules?" Adam asked.

"Well, test subjects or rather 'patients' are different from nurses. Nurses tend to be a little more expendable than you guys simply because we've already fulfilled our purpose.

"Once the doctor feels that you've essentially given him enough 'data' as he calls it, he promotes you to a third-class nurse."

Atreus's explanation baffled Adam as his body shivered due to his exposed bare skin. He quickly dressed himself and sat on the bed listening to Atreus attentively.

"Sevant was a second-class nurse like me. He enjoyed the pleasantries that came with the title, so to speak. We all have our own room and a request sheet. Every month, the doctor looks at all the request sheets and pulls a few strings and for the most part, grants our wishes so long as we stay within the facility and fall in line."

Adam quickly cut off Atreus from his explanation.

"So, this place is a facility? Where are we?"

Atreus let out a big sigh and walked over toward the fridge, grabbed a canned beverage and sat across from Adam on the bed. Opening the can and taking a few sips, Atreus watched as Adam stared at him inquisitively, waiting for his reply.

"Look, Adam. Before I say anything else, I need you to know something. Do as the doctor orders, and you will live, and things might get easier, but if you try to rebel…"

Atreus paused and took a sip of his drink. "You will always suffer."

"So why do you do it then?" Adam asked. "If it's making you suffer, then why…"

Atreus looked at Adam and shrugged his shoulders.

"Because I'm numb."

"Numb?" Adam asked in confusion. "How can you be numb from being tortured and watching people die left, right and center? What about having to kill someone in cold blood just so you can live?" Adam yelled in anger as his tears surfaced.

Atreus looked up toward the ceiling and closed his eyes.

"Because I know I'll never leave this place. No one ever will. So, you have to grow numb, Adam, or your mind will never cope with it, never grown to handle everything it sees."

Adam's face sank as he shook his head in defiance.

"You may think that, but not me. I'll be the one to get out. You just wait and see," Adam yelled with fake confidence. "Fuck this place, and fuck… fuck everything within it."

Ignoring Adam's remark, Atreus continued. "Adam, maybe I thought like that many years ago. But if you don't adapt, if you don't ignore the pain and the suffering then you'll become mad. Living like this and accepting it as normalcy is the healthiest thing you can do in this place."

Adam couldn't believe what Atreus was saying. It was beyond his comprehension.

"Accepting your fate as an expendable tool for a lunatic?"

"As I was saying, once you become a third-class nurse, you do all the maintenance and upkeep of this facility. Essentially, you're a slave. Generally, your duties involve general maintenance, cultivating indoor crops, and assisting the technicians who keep this place afloat. If you do well and an opening is available, you can become a second-class like me, with a request sheet and your own living space. We 'take care' of the test subjects i.e., the patients.

"As for first-class nurses, there are only two at the moment, and they don't just get a room, they get to live outside the facility."

Adam's eyebrows raised as if Atreus had said the first-class nurses grew wings and flew free.

"What do you mean, outside?" Adam said in a perplexed tone.

It was obvious but his mind refused to believe it. It wasn't—couldn't be—possible, could it?

Atreus finished his beverage and threw it in the trash bin over with his cart near the entrance he through which he had come.

"Right now, we are deep underground, beneath an island not shown on any maps of any kind. Only a select few individuals in the world know of its existence and it doesn't help either that this particular island is so far apart from civilization, it takes about a month or so just to get supplies shipped here. If you become a first-class nurse, you can live outside on the island, you see?

"They only come here for routine medical checks on second and third-class nurses. Third-class nurses maintain the facility, while second-class nurses are assigned a patient to take care of—and I say 'take care of' very loosely. Finally, first-class care for all the nurses below them."

Atreus walked to the cart having finished his explanation, allowing Adam to contemplate on what he had just heard. He smiled for a while and looked up toward Atreus.

"So, there is a way out of here after all?" Adam said and Atreus rolled his eyes.

"You know something? You remind me so much of Sevant when he was young."

Adam's eyes darted toward Atreus and stared daggers at him.

"Don't compare me to that asshole."

Atreus chuckled. "Don't be misled. He started out just like you, but this place warped his mind. Instead of ignoring or casting away his gaze, he embraced this place because he had to.

"He was on his way to becoming a first-class nurse until you came along."

"How would you even know what he was like when he was young?"

"Adam, I've been here for over thirty years; Sevant and I were only about your age when we were patients." Adam's hand rose to his mouth and a cold sweat was forming across his face.

"You've been in here for *thirty years?*" Adam replied in disbelief.

"Yes, Sevant and I met each other once we fulfilled our duties as patients and became nurses," Atreus said fondly. "I remember his attitude, brash and ready to fight anyone. But unfortunately, as soon as the doctor demonstrated his control over this place, Sevant folded.

"I guess the only difference between you both might be that you're not willing to fold yet. I heard what happened between the two of you, that he kept beating you over and over much worse than what the doctor would typically do for such minor or nonexistent offenses.

"Yet instead of caving in and falling into despair, you just killed him outright when the opportunity struck," Atreus said.

Adam stood up from the bed, needing Atreus to hear and understand his plight more than ever. "Look, I never wanted to kill Sevant! Over and over, I kept crying and wishing for the beatings to just stop. The only way I knew how was to end him permanently!"

Adam was in a state of anguish.

Atreus looked at Adam and smirked. "Then why did you dirty your hands then? Sevant would have died had you left him alone with the poison, wouldn't he?"

Adam took a step back.

"Because he kept calling out to me."

"So, he calls you. You help him, giving him false hope. Then repeatedly stab him, making sure he feels agonizing pain before he died? That was to help him, was it?"

"No, you're right. I was angry," Adam stated reluctantly. "I'd lost all sense of reality by then, just trying to save myself, save my own skin. My mind snapped when he started begging for his life. As if he deserved to be saved after what he'd done! I'd never heard anything so egocentric!

"So I lost control," Adam stated in admission.

"Then you both were not all that different at all, were you? Hopefully, however, you might be able to keep a level head and not fall into madness like he did," Atreus said.

"Were you and Sevant close?" Adam asked with curiosity.

"Well, according to the doctor, he was my biological brother," Atreus stated bluntly.

Adam visibly recoiled, the statement sending him reeling.

He couldn't believe this man was related to that piece of garbage. And despite that, Atreus was seeking to give Adam somewhat of a reassurance that he had no ill will toward him.

"Listen kid, I can see that what I've just told you has troubled you. between you and me, I shan't be losing any sleep over the matter of his death, and neither should you.

"The man who died by your hands wasn't my brother. That was just his shell. He used to be my best friend and he did in fact help me and the other nurses when we tried to escape. However, after that incident, he changed and that is when the man I knew…"

Atreus paused, clearing his throat as a hint of emotion came shimmering through. "No, that is when the brother I knew died. I don't blame you, Adam," Atreus said. "I sure enough am no better than he was either. It was as if the world forsook us, so hell took us in."

With a sideways glance, Atreus collected all his things, taking any trash in sight and slowly walked out of Adam's new room, leaving him alone to his thoughts once again.

Chapter 6

Humans are so fragile yet so remarkable once they've been broken, or rather awakened. When the mind is left in a dark place with no hope of salvation, it begins to falter yet also sheds its excess weight of worry. That darkness collides with the mind, slowly chipping away at society's term known as *sanity,* making suffering and pain an ordeal leading to salvation.

Murder, rape, torture, and all other forms of degrading humiliation are just tools to awaken people. Life's insignificance becomes significant when these tools eradicate the instincts of man, cleansing the mind in blood and fear in order to progress forward to true freedom.

The shackles of morality bind mankind, and the only way to remove them is to tear out society's pathetic influence. The cure to a meaningless existence is simply having man groping for sanity and wanting to retch until he spills his guts, reduced to being a void inside of himself.

***

Adam awoke with an awkward sense of calm. Rising from the bed and scratching his scalp, he wondered why he felt so accustomed today. He knew a new test was going to arrive and of course, the fear of pain and or death was there too, the same way it always was.

However, Adam felt a sense of clarity on this morning, finally having a means of understanding what this place was. Hope was welling up within him.

Jogging on the spot, Adam wondered what the next test would be.

As his thoughts continued, he came to grips with the realization that so far, things did not look promising, so Adam attempted to calm his nerves by exercising, tossing his anger and his frustrations away with each push-up, great beads of sweat dripping from his nose.

Yet as time progressed, his nerves were tightening, almost molding into a hard-pressed block of steel. "Proceed to the next testing area, Adam," the doctor's voice insisted, breaking out in a loud volume. Adam jolted and grasped onto his chest, breathing heavily. The noise had startled him so much, all the mental strength he had formed giving way.

Even though each new room became slightly more bearable, one thing Adam wished for was that the doctor's voice would change slightly. It was really grating, and he just hoped that the tone would change the further he progressed. The door unlocked and its hinges shrieked as it opened. Adam looked for Atreus to see if he was on the other side, but no one was there.

It was as if the room itself was inviting Adam deep into its bowels. The room was pitch black and a warm air brushed Adam's face with a smell so putrid, it buckled his knees, forcing Adam to cover his mouth as he coughed erratically. On top of this, the doctor's voice broke out anew.

"Adam, enter the room within five seconds or you will be terminated."

The voice was colder than before, unamused and sterner. Holding his nostrils, Adam entered the darkness that called out to him, the door slamming shut behind him as soon as he cleared it.

Adam could not see a single shred of light and no matter how much he adjusted his eyes, the darkness was perpetual, a never-ending abyss of black.

The smell only grew even stronger with every step he took forward, the air thick and putrid. Adam was struggling to keep his innards in check.

"Adam, stretch out your arm and search for the light switch ahead of you," said the doctor. Following his instructions, Adam aimlessly outstretched his hand in search for a switch, covering his mouth with the other. His fingers brushed against something soft yet damp, and he took a step forward again to get a firm grasp of whatever this was. His breathing became more frantic and unsteady while his bare feet could now feel a dampness, a liquid that was oddly familiar to him.

His hand quivered as he felt flesh and liquid dripping over his skin. Finally, a hard surface almost like a block had been placed in a bag of meat. His fingers felt it. He could feel the switch.

As Adam flipped it, a beam of light blinded his eyes and forced him to take a few steps back.

Once his eyes adjusted, Adam's mind was tearing itself apart.

Atreus's lifeless body lay before him, propped up onto a metal pike piercing his upper back, and a large car battery had been rammed into his chest cavity, a great bundle of multicolored wires sprawling out of his nostrils. His mouth was wide open with a light bulb shining within it.

Sections of his teeth had been torn free and his tongue appeared to have been sliced away.

In place of Atreus's eyes were star-shaped bulbs with blood dripping out of his sockets, resembling the tears of sorrow of a man trapped in chaos.

Smaller light fixtures sprawled everywhere, stapled all across his naked body. The blood had puddled up beneath his dangling feet, his hands covering his ears.

"What the fuck!" Adam said as he continued to examine the body.

Two metal spikes pierced through his hands and into his skull to keep them in place.

Adam's intense panic broke out and he vomited in a nearby corner away from the blood and grotesque imagery. Atreus's insides were spilling out across the floor, reminding Adam of what he had just witnessed, causing a never-ending loop of nausea and disgust.

The doctor's face grinned as he saw Adam's reaction from within his private locale, staring at the screen and monitoring Adam's every movement as he typed endlessly onto a worn keyboard.

"What do you think of that?" the doctor said. "You have ten minutes to find the key card for the next room. I'll make it slightly easier for you this time. All you need to know is that the key card is located somewhere within that husk of meat," said the doctor with a menacing tone. "See, I'm even giving you clues now."

Adam dropped down to his knees, staring at the ground.

"Why? Why did you do this to him?" Adam said, his voice filled with immeasurable sorrow. "He was the only one who treated me like I was a person and not some lab rat!"

As if that should have made a difference to whether the doctor slaughtered Atreus or not.

The man had no humanity; Adam had already known at, but his mind didn't wish to accept it.

The tears dripped off his face, falling onto the cold hard floor. Adam's wails ringed within the room as he made the mistake of looking back at the corpse.

Grasping the hairs on his head, his cries grew more frantic and desperate.

"Someone. Dear God. Help me. Help me. Someone, please, anyone!"

"The penalty for not finding it within the allotted time is the removal of four fingers from your left hand," the doctor said. "Unfortunately, you don't get to choose which hand, so I insist it'll be four fingers from the left. Quite specific, don't you think?"

Adam still could not fully register what was occurring and in the moment, felt as if a thousand knives were slowly injecting themselves into his skull.

His mind was falling apart due to the images replaying in his head.

The grotesque nature of it all, the sharp pang of guilt, and—of course—the loss of an ally weighed heavily upon Adam's shoulders.

His face exuded tears and snot dribbling over his mouth, hacking over the smell of the body.

"You won't get away with this, you piece of shit!" Adam yelled, his cheeks red, teeth grating against one another. "I'll find you, and I'll make sure you suffer a slow and painful death. I swear, I'll… I'll make you beg me and more. Fuck your tests and fuck you!"

"Come, come, Adam. Your test begins, now," the doctor said in an indifferent and merciless tone. Adam sat next to the door, trying to pry it open every so often.

Grasping his hands, he eyed how feeble he was, then was groveling on the ground, wishing this would all emerge to have been nothing more than a terrible nightmare.

Yet it was certainly not a nightmare; this was his reality of pain, humiliation, and helplessness. This was Adam's world and the one to which he now belonged.

He tried to remember better times and pleasanter thoughts, such as who his father and mother were. What was his hobby? Where had he been born? Yet Adam knew his life had never been like this, and that before all this, he had a family, friends, and maybe even a companion back home. However, his mind filled itself with blurry figures of people, places, and things.

Slowly, but not frequently enough, things would come in here and there but overall, nothing he could follow. The aroma of decaying flesh, however, became more prevalent as Adam calmed himself, forcing him to remove his shirt as he firmly wrapped it around his mouth and nose.

"One minute warning, Adam. I suggest you at least try. There is still time. If you do not comply with this test, the penalty will most surely be dealt upon you. Why worry about a dead man when you must cling to survival? Do you think this will be the end, Adam?

"I have just started to gain valuable information from you and now you refuse to comply. Think of it this way, you little worm," the doctor said in annoyance. "If you simply follow all my directions to the letter, maybe things may turn out well for you. As you already know, I have the need of qualified nurses and two spots are now vacant because of you.

"So why not do as you're told? Once I'm bored of you, you'll have a much better life from then on. Now go ahead and find that key card." The doctor clearly was obsessed with these so-called 'tests.' So much so, that he was trying to rationalize with Adam in the moment.

"Why did you kill him?" Adam screeched as he ignored the doctor's reply.

He pulled his shirt ever so slightly to peek clearly at Atreus's mangled body posed in such a mocking fashion that the sheer sight of it made his weeping gather strength.

"Only fifteen seconds are remaining, Adam. What a waste of time you have caused today."

Adam fell silent and waited by the door, still hunched over, glancing at his feet wet with Atreus's blood. A faint glimmer of hope the day before now lay shattered by cruel realities.

"Oh dear. The time has now concluded," the doctor said. "As of now, I will be sending in your new nurse. Please return to your quarters." The door's lock clicked, and Adam could now open the door. The air was clean and no longer humid. Adam walked over to the shower head and began turning the valve to pour water down his head. Nothing came out.

He walked toward the fridge to look for something to drink yet the fridge filled to the brim yesterday was now empty in entirety.

Adam was gradually understanding the doctor's petty nature.

"How sick do you have to be to put people through this?" Adam yelled out in anger.

"As I recall, you ungrateful little wretch, I clearly told you before to mind your tone with me," the doctor said with anger and contempt, his voice booming over the intercom. "You're lucky to still be alive. Note that I have terminated others for much less."

Adam sat on the bed, looking at the trail of red footprints smeared across the floor.

"You kidnap people, strap them to a bed and then torture them as soon as they wake up. How do you live with yourself?" Adam questioned in a low defeated voice.

"Adam, you are missing the point. My research here is groundbreaking. It will shake the world to its very core, and you are a part of that. You are taking a prime position in one of the world's most impactful experiments; you are making history! There, isn't that good, Adam?

"One day, my research will complete and the world as we know it will experience a drastic change, in which man finally transcends meaninglessness," the doctor said with zeal and pride.

"What is man's meaninglessness?"

Adam was humoring the doctor as he slid against the wall to the floor.

"Life itself! Adam, whether we live or die, there is nothing for us at the end—but was there ever really anything for man to begin with? Mother Nature made a mistake and now man's self-awareness is his biggest curse. Yet I can make Mother Nature herself bend to my whims and thus with that power, I will remake the world. Governments, society, collectivism, etc.

"It is all a sham; man should look to the past, not the future. We should analyze and see how our primal instincts fare against ongoing threats. Once we have eradicated man's instincts and society's moral dogma, then there is a future. No price is too great for my ambition, so if I must mutilate and kill one of my top nurses to be able make a point, then so be it."

The doctor's reply sent shivers down Adam's spine. He couldn't follow any of it. It felt as if these were the ramblings of a madman, a lunatic only just tethered to reality.

"So, you kill people to benefit mankind? That doesn't seem

counter-intuitive to you at all?"

The doctor's zeal and enthusiasm extinguished themselves in a flash.

"Well, I wouldn't expect an ingrate like you to understand," he said.

The door from the previous trial opened and three tall men walked inside in unison. One was pushing a cart with tools all jingling and clapping against one another as the cart pushed forward.

Adam stood in haste, scuttling to the other end of the room.

"Get away from me!" The men began setting up their contraption next to Adam's bed.

Sevant was a mere elf compared to these behemoths.

A dark-skinned man with scars across his face and a large overbite sat on the bed in a nonchalant fashion, sharpening a blade with a wet stone.

The other two were both light skinned with scars across their arms, yet their faces for the most part were untouched. However, upon closer inspection as they were removing objects from the cart, their pant legs rose and revealed that the creatures were not of human flesh.

Instead, both these men must have had their original legs removed at some point and now the only things left were these prosthetics. Adam braced himself against the wall prepared for a fight, knowing full well the odds stacked high against him.

The doctor's voice spoke out.

"So then, Adam. I will remove four fingers from your hand. Your left hand. However, I have been feeling a little generous as of late. I have managed to relieve most of my stress in the latest art piece I created, and I am very much worried that your performance will suffer a hindrance.

"So, comply and walk over to these fine gentlemen and take your penalty. If you are able to do so with no defiance whatsoever, I will have your fingers reattached."

There was a pause—no doubt another episode of psychological torture.

"Now, if you decide to give them a hard time, create a fight and cause a scene, then I will have these men go through a bit of irony. As you can see, those two men were in the same situation as you, yet they decided to rebel. To go against my wishes is to harm yourself. They are now third-class nurses, permanently. They will never progress past that level either.

"For you, see, even if you comply from now on and pass all these tests, if you dare try my patience a few too many times… Well then, I'll see to it that the remainder of your days will be as dull and restrictive as these fools'. Yet look at my dear Luke. A class act this one, on his way to becoming first class, in fact. He has two lackeys to do all his dirty work, and all his appendages are intact. Adam, try to be a Luke, compliant and thorough. That's all I ask."

The two handicapped men had visibly angered faces. They did not want to be here whatsoever, yet here they were, doing the doctor's bidding as best as they could.

After seeing the pain Atreus had been through, he couldn't blame them.

Luke, on the other hand, had a flat expression, almost mechanical, with his dead eyes staring directly at the sharp edge of the blade. The sound of the knife drawing over and over against the firm stone was testing Adam's resolve. Back and forth it went in a well-drilled motion.

Adam's heart pounded, the sweat from his brow flowing endlessly. He felt an excruciating pain developing within his head, like a massive migraine coming on and his palms were cold to the touch. He placed his fingers in his ears to stop the unbearable noise.

Finally, Luke stopped, looking at the blade, twisting it ever so slightly.

He was inspecting every nook and cranny.

"Place your hand in the cart, Adam. Comply with me from now on and try to complete your tests in earnest, or I'll have your limbs removed," the doctor said. Adam's face flushed as he stared at the two other men, searching their faces for empathy, looking for any emotion he might exploit. Yet as they made eye contact, he could see nothing but their desperation.

They were almost begging Adam to comply.

They did not want to fight, nor did they want to cut off his legs, but they were dead set on listening to the doctor's demands, no matter what those might be.

Reluctantly, Adam walked toward the bed and sat right next to the cart, placing his left arm flat on the cart with his fingers pointed forward.

The two other men beside Luke grabbed a rubber stick and asked him to bite onto it as the procedure moved forward. Adam complied and placed the rubber between his jaws.

He clamped down. These two men were now holding Adam in place.

One was holding his arm steady, and the other towering over him, pushing his hands against Adam's shoulders to keep him unflinching. Luke stood up and for a moment, began looking into his eyes. "Don't move." These were the only words Adam heard before he saw the blade pressing against his pinky finger. The blade joined forces with Adam's flesh as the skin, muscle, and bone all sung in harmony, Adam's eyes rolled back as his teeth clenched and bore down upon the rubber stick in his mouth, heaving and screaming in agony.

The crunching from the bones was loud and Adam soaked in every decibel of his own screams, his arms and legs restless now, taking every ounce of his mental capacity to stay as still as possible. He outright refused to lose either of his legs and by the end of it, all he knew was that the doctor would keep his word. So, he pressed on with sheer will and determination.

By mistake, Adam then looked at his hand covered in blood, realizing the severity of the situation. What appeared to be an eternity of anguish for him was really just the beginning. He still had three fingers left. Adam's eyes were moist with tears, his face red, and his body shaking.

He looked at his feeble little finger dangling by just a sliver of tissue as Luke ripped the remainder of it off, leaving a nub of open flesh, spilling his blood all over the cart. The bright red substance then was leaving a trail across the cart's side, sliding along its edge with a slow yet steady flow in continuous supply. Adam closed his eyes as he attempted to remove his mind from his body in an effort to avoid the pain. It didn't prove useful in the slightest.

Adam could feel the blade's love for his fingers as it became intimate with every layer of skin and bone through which it tore. The blood was fresh and hot, coating Adam's palms with its warm embrace. Before Adam could register the loss of the next finger, he could feel that there was only one more left. Just like that, darkness was filling his mind.

He welcomed it with open arms.

The shock passed through his body and entered Adam's mind. Nothingness had never felt so pleasurable. Adam's head sank over his shoulders as he had passed out from the pain.

Luke removed the last finger, then proceeded to wipe the blade down with an alcohol-covered rag. The two third-class nurses were astonished at Adam's resilience. This young man had actually sat completely still as all his fingers were lopped off one after the other.

Even after becoming unconscious, his body stayed still as they dressed his wounds.

"Looks like we get to put them back on, yeah?"

The other man simply gave a half-cocked smile and grabbed the stitching kit. Luke placed his precious knife in its proper place within the cart and walked toward the door.

"Oh, by the way, Luke!" the doctor called out.

"Yes, Doctor?" Luke said, staring at the door handle.

"Adam is your new patient. I trust you won't be as intrusive as the others?"

"No, Doctor," Luke stated plainly.

"You see, this is why you're one of my favorites, Luke. You were such a wonderful patient and you're now a perfect nurse. I'll tell you I might need you to stay in second class a bit longer given what pathetic saps I have been working with as of late."

Luke looked toward a corner of the room, knowing the camera was there and with a blank stare, Luke's monotone voice made the other two nurses shiver.

"Yes, Doctor," Luke replied.

"Do you think I am not of sound mind? Do you believe all my doctorates are merely for show? I have one of the highest rated intelligence quotients ever recorded in history.

"My contributions to this world have shaped the very fabric of modern medicine.

"My engineering skills have no equal and my latest projects have pushed humanity's technological advancements decades ahead of their time. I am evolution's messiah, born to rule the weaker batch of apes on this small rock on which we all live. Questioning my very authority is questioning the very laws of nature. My word is absolute, and my will supersedes all others' endeavors. Yet your mind that is as feeble as our primitive cousins questions me?

"It is society at large that is ill. They stick to their tradition, to their pathetic rules of order and 'natural law.' When insanity is sanity and sanity is insanity, why would I ever follow suit?

"The world at large lives in delusion. Yet I am wide awake, ready to awaken man.

"Those refusing to embrace enlightenment serve only one purpose, that of my amusement."

A sharp pain surged through Adam's body. Lying in bed motionless, he attempted to move his fingers. Immediate panic struck him. He could not feel a single one.

He jumped from the bed and pulled out his left hand from the sheets in quick desperation. Then came a large rush of relief. All his fingers were intact, simply wrapped in bandages covering his whole hand. The doctor's voice chimed in as Adam stared at his hand.

"You received clean cuts through and through, so attaching your nerves as well as your tissue was a fairly easy procedure. However, I doubt you'll be able to feel anything for a long while."

Adam stayed silent, waiting for the doctor's next demands.

"So, Adam. You must complete the test by searching for the key card within Atreus's corpse. If you fail yet again, your fingers are not the only appendages that shall be removed."

Adam clambered up from the bed, walked toward the door and waited for the doctor to open it. The wave of a putrid stench bursting through the door's cracks no longer fazed Adam, and he walked into the darkness with an uninterested expression.

As the door closed behind him, the outer edges of the blood puddles were coagulating.

The floor gripped his feet with each step because of the glue-like residue the blood had left.

"Your test begins now," the doctor stated, and Adam held his breath. Walking over to the corpse's location, he outstretched his hand, searching for the switch. The lights flickered on and there before him was Atreus, still naked, mangled and modified with wires and lights.

He set off walking around the body, searching for any obvious signs of an incision or stitched area, in the hope it concealed the key card. But it was so difficult with the amount of *surgery*, or butchery more like, that it was a pointless exercise. Time was running out for him.

Deep down, Adam knew the doctor wouldn't make it that easy for him, which meant that he would have stuffed the key card deeper within Atreus's body. Without hesitation, and now without a choice, he pried the fingers from his right hand upward, into the body's anus.

Turning away, Adam carefully worked his fingers in and lo and behold, he felt something just as his whole hand entered the corpse. "You sick fuck!"

Adam's face was in pure disgust, but the time was ticking by, and he could no longer afford to be shy. Whatever it was, he needed to remove it.

What else could it be? It had to be the key card.

Managing to grip the object, he began pulling it out, revealing a plastic bag covered in feces. As his hand pulled out of the anal canal, feces spilled out of the body, leaving Adam's bare hand and the floor tainted. He coughed using his left arm as a buffer between himself and the smell.

Walking over to the door, he thought he had achieved the task but instead, as he opened the bag, only a folded piece of paper was inside. He opened it, reading its contents to himself.

'Hey Adam, you're probably flipping out right about now.' That very sentence let Adam crack a smile. 'So, I can tell where things are headed; he's done this a few times to the others. He's always had a grudge with me, and me helping you was the straw that broke the camel's back. I used to think that I'd do anything for survival, but I guess this was it for me.

'I was tired, couldn't do this anymore. So, I helped you instead of myself. Thought that in some way, I could make up for all the harm I've done. I'm pretty certain I'm going to hell but maybe its denizens might take it easy on me if I fuck up the asshole's test.

"The key card will be in my ball sack. What he wants from you is to dig into my corpse and not find it, then he'll cut off your fingers.'

A little too late for that, Adam thought and continued to read the note.

'There should be some stitching underneath my scrotum. If by some miracle you do ever get the chance, please kill him. And when I say kill him, I mean make him feel as much agony and pain as possible. Good luck and please send him my regards.'

The doctor nearly crashed his face against the screen trying to see what Adam had removed from the body's anal cavity. He was mumbling a gibberish to himself with the occasional slur as he typed on his computer keyboard. Adam reached toward the scrotum.

Sure enough, the stitches were there. Digging into the flesh and finally removing the key card, Adam could not help himself from laughing hysterically as he walked over to the door and swiped the key card across the scanner. The test was complete.

The doctor's face was bright red, bashing his keyboard against the monitor over and over again. "That piece of scum gave him the answer! Even in his death, he still mocks me!"

The doctor stormed out of his office, opening the door and slamming it behind him.

Chapter 7

Adam's new room was wall to wall white. *As always,* he thought. *I guess a white room is easier to clean up the blood, shit, piss and puke.* He glanced around, noticing he now had a bed, a full-sized fridge, a desk with a microwave, an actual bathroom, and even a walk-in closet with several pairs of the same clothing as he currently wore, with, of course, the doctor's emblem emblazoned on them. Opening the fridge, Adam had a sensory overload.

Sodas, juice, water, and plenty of microwaveable meals.

Adam was shocked and elated. *All these goods just for me,* he thought.

Walking over to the bathroom, although there was no door, Adam found he now had a clear shower curtain. He thought again that with each test passed, the following room would have a slightly more comfortable appeal. Whether that be a fridge full of soda, or even a basic item like a shower curtain, he would have gained some type of added comfort.

Yes, he agreed the shower curtain wasn't a biggie, but thinking back to room one or even room two, where he had next to nothing, he greatly appreciated the addition of this basic item. *Some semblance of privacy is better than none,* he thought.

Below the sink were two boxes of bars of soap and toilet paper.

Again, more items Adam believed most would class as 'everyday essentials,' and they probably were. But to go without such for some time made you appreciate them far more.

Now, a toilet roll was a thing of wonder and magnificence.

So, yes, Adam could wipe his ass the way he believed most did, and the way he deserved—with toilet paper, and he could scrub his body with soap, ridding his skin, his nails, his hair—especially his nasal hair—of the putrid gore and lingering stench clinging to his worn body.

He smiled, turned on the shower, and grabbed a bar of soap, savoring the warm water cascading over his body. Adam's flesh felt the downpour of heated water melting away his fatigue, but the pain in his left hand was awakening. Most likely, whatever sedative they had given him was now wearing off, and applying hot water was not doing him any favors.

The bandages had been wrapped so tightly that his fingers were all pointed at attention, fixed rigid. He laughed within himself as he now had a perpetual karate chop at his disposal.

Adam could faintly remember watching late-night movies with his father, most of which were karate films; the man seemed to have an obsession with that genre of cinema. His heart elevated slightly, and his chest ached. His father. Yes, his father. How could he have forgotten?

Thinking about those nights threaded Adam's memories together bit by bit, one vague recollection slowly resurfacing and leading onto another, then to the next.

Although not clear, they were enough to convince Adam that whatever had happened to him over the time he had been at the facility, he had once been in a more civilized place before.

Even holding a bar of soap triggered something deep in his memory.

Try as he might, he couldn't remember the intricate details of his father's face, but the figure seemed to be there at all times he sought it, although reduced to a blurred image.

It was also the sensation of having a father or a parent, that of not knowing abandonment or aloneness, a sense of heartfelt belonging— something for which he had yearned.

Adam's realization gave him a new form of despair. "I have a family. *Do* I still have a family?" he spoke softly. "And where are they?" He wondered if his father was looking for him. *Does Dad know I was kidnapped or worse, perhaps? Does Dad believe me to be dead?*

Clenching his right hand into a fist, Adam banged it against the shower wall yelling incoherently. "It's not fair. This just isn't fucking fair! How can the bastards do this to me—not only to me, but to my dad as well! Torturing people like this! *Un-fucking-fair!*"

Adam shouted his new invented word repeatedly before slipping, falling onto the tub's floor.

He now experienced loss yet again. Uncanny, wasn't it? Not moments ago, he didn't even know if he had a father at all and now, his heart ached after remembering better times.

He was recollecting something so peaceful, far off away from the world he was a part of now.

After staying there motionless for what seemed hours, Adam stood, turning off the shower head and changed into a brand-new pair of *embossed* clothing.

Looking at the emblem bothered him greatly, a deep, disturbing ache.

So, they have branded me now, have they?

They are treating me like cattle or a head of steer.

Before any more thoughts could run through his mind, the doctor's voice boomed out through the speaker. "Adam, I will be giving your next test to you shortly, and Luke will now be your new nurse. I cannot believe how particular you are, Adam. Maybe you two will be the perfect fit." The doctor's laugh became more pronounced and erratic.

"Third time's a charm! Are you familiar with that saying, Adam?"

And just like that, the voice disappeared, followed by total silence. Adam quickly grabbed several frozen meals, three beverages and a bottle of water from the fridge.

Checking each meal, he unpacked them, heating them separately in the microwave at three minutes apiece. His head was throbbing as he could tell this play of events was a familiar routine back home. "Wherever home was," he thought aloud.

After a few hours, Adam could see the testing door give way as it slid open.

Out came Luke with his own cart and there in full sight, the knife he'd used to cut off Adam's appendages, lying upright in a small pedestal.

Luke was silent as he grabbed the remains of Adam's banquet, throwing them in a bin within the cart and he continued on with a check list, inspecting the room all over. Luke's face was scarred far worse than Atreus's and his build made Sevant look like a child.

It appeared the further Adam progressed, the rooms, facilities and niceties were all increasing but unfortunately for Adam, the standard of *nurse* also increased. And not in a caring way but growing far more competent at what they could do. Standing at what must have been seven foot tall, Luke only had a few inches of height to spare from constantly hitting his head on the ceiling.

Adam waited for a snide remark or maybe if he was lucky, something that made him feel as if Atreus wasn't the only pure soul within this place.

Yet no response came back as if he didn't even exist. Adam didn't mind this; however, he wouldn't dare attempt to speak up in front of this monster of a human being.

This guy was gargantuan and could and would surely tear Adam apart if given the opportunity. Luke proceeded to gather all of his cleaning supplies and made sure every nook and cranny of the room looked clean, even as far as making Adam's bed, forcing Adam to sit on the floor. *I wonder will he scrub my back?* Adam thought, but quickly erased it from his mind.

He probably would have obliged but surely would've replaced soap and sponge with a sandblaster. After Luke finished, he gathered his tools and placed them away neatly and orderly into the cart and walked back from whence he came, closing the door behind him.

"Adam, the test is ready. Please proceed through the next door," the doctor said abruptly as his voice echoed in the room. Adam pressed forward, feeling a hint of the numbness of which Atreus spoke. At this point, there may have been more ludicrous obstacles ahead, but if he simply took this as the day to day, he may keep his sanity intact.

Sounded easy, but it would certainly test any human being's resolve.

The automatic door slammed shut behind him and as always, the unexpected became the expected. Adam stood still for a minute as his eyes attempted to register what his mind couldn't, two women and two men standing in plain sight, not a single shred of clothing between them to conceal their exposure to the elements.

Adam's eyes averted from them as he blushed slightly at the sight of the women. An unknown yet familiar feeling of distress flushed over him. Keeping his composure, Adam's eyes threw away their modesty as he examined these four individuals to figure out the test's intended goal. And, as if by magic…

"Adam, your test this round is fairly simple. Converse with each individual, one at a time. It's up to you who you start with but after having a *chat* with the four, you will then decide who will live and who will die." Immediately, Luke approached Adam and gave him a small electronic transmitter with four switches labeled with letters.

"Note that one of the individuals is a convicted felon who was supposed to be executed a few months ago. *He* or *she* is a serial killer. I was actually somewhat fond of their work."

A white screen slowly slid toward the floor, hiding the other four behind it. The screen then displayed horrific images of mutilated men and women.

Some of the images displayed corpses lying side to side stitched against one another, showing pictures of dismembered parts of human flesh stuffed inside of a chest cavity.

There was a picture of a woman with her breasts cut off, replaced with pools of blood all over her body. The corpse had been fashioned to hold something in her arms and upon closer inspection, she was clutching a doll depicting an infant with its eyes plucked out.

Adam turned his head away from the screen, no longer able to bear witnessing such horrors. He couldn't stomach it. Seeing Atreus had been bad enough, but this was on another level.

"If you do happen to kill the felon outright, the others will be set free, no harm no foul. The other three are just innocent bystanders. Well, to be more precise, they are the relatives of those who have crossed me as of late, so smile today, Adam, because you will be on a secure live feed for those pathetic ingrates. Make it a good show, Adam," the doctor said with glee.

"You have an hour to make your choice. If the hour is up and the felon is still not dead, then you have failed this test. If no one else is alive but the felon, you have also failed this test. Failing this test will result in a very painful endeavor."

"Like what?" Adam spoke calmly.

"Now, that, Adam, is a surprise. But as you have seen, I always deliver," said the doctor in anticipation. "The test begins now."

The screen lifted away from the floor, revealing the naked individuals once more. Adam was perplexed since at face value, each one of them seemed incapable of such atrocities.

The two men were standing tall but visibly distressed and the two women were fighting the urge to cover themselves as if someone had ordered them to stand firm without regard for their current predicament. Adam walked closer, trying desperately to focus in on their faces rather than their bare bodies exposed for all to see.

He started with the furthest gentleman on the left, one who was rather frail, but extremely tall. His body was lanky and somewhat flabby—a walking contradiction in the flesh, a cartoon-like human with amber-like skin who carried himself with dignity, as if a man of nobility.

"Err. Hi, I'm Adam. What's your name?"

As if a weight had been lifted from his shoulders, the man began speaking with conviction.

"This guy is fucking insane. My dad's company went ahead and funded this moron and once my father found out this shit, he pulled the funding! He's a fucking lunatic, Aaron—"

"Adam. My name's Adam!"

"Sorry, Adam. Anyway, I went out clubbing with my boys, as you do. We were dancing, having a good time, and then nothing. Got black-out drunk and now I'm here! Can't remember much after that. Next thing I knew, this fucktard woke me up. I was fucking naked in the middle of this hell hole." The fog of mystery was now clear, and Adam could tell whatever thoughts he had were shut down in front of him. The man was more of a petulant spoiled man-child, having been fed with a silver spoon since birth. Adam could already feel the doctor's rage begin to boil.

The man was pointing at Luke, spewing slur after slur. The doctor's voice appeared once again. "I was very clear that you were only allowed to speak to Adam until he attempted to converse with you, and under the stipulation that you answered his question first!" The doctor yelled. "Now, tell him your name, or I'll have Luke carve out your tongue!"

The young adult took a step back but refused to comply.

"Fuck you, sick fuck. My dad will own your old ass when he finds out what you did to me."

This guy has no idea who or what he is dealing with, Adam thought. Better to comply and silently make a plan of attack than to outright refuse the doctor.

Looking at his hand as a cautionary tale, Adam spoke out to save this man.

"Stop it! Just tell me your name. I just need to pass this test and all of you, besides the murderer, get to go home! The man may be insane, but he keeps his word, so please, just give me some time."

The other three were still silent yet visibly stressed and afraid. For a moment, the young man stopped, looked at Adam and leaned in close to his face.

"Who the fuck do you think you are?" the young man said as he spat on Adam's face. "I don't have to do shit! I swear, if you don't get me out of here right this instant, my dad will have your neck! I will..." His voice stopped as a seven-foot-tall behemoth strangled his neck as though it was a straw. He may have been a few heads above Adam in terms of height, but Luke was in a league of his own, bashing his giant fist against the young man, throwing him across the room.

The young man wobbled to his feet coughing and shaking.

"What the fuck!" he yelled as tears trickled from the corners of his eyes. He stuck his fingers in his mouth, feeling around to notice that several teeth were missing from his lower jaw.

Luke did not stop there, however. He walked over with an almost mechanical stride.

"Get the fuck away from me!" the young man screamed. Luke pinned the young man down to the ground with ease, as if the battered man-child were a defenseless infant and held him in place with his own weight, firmly clenching the fool's torso with his knees.

There it is, Adam thought, as the blade appeared before Luke's hand, grasping it with such strength that his veins bulged. "No, please don't. I'll listen, man. I'll listen!"

Luke had no signs of emotion whatsoever, simply a cold dead stare of indifference. To Luke, the doctor's orders were absolute. He was a tool to use according to the doctor's bidding and so far, it seemed Luke intended to follow through with the doctor's orders.

No amount of begging would prevent Luke from carrying out his will. Prying the young man's mouth open like a clam, Luke slowly pushed his knife into his mouth. The man was coughing and wheezing, wailing and screaming as his mouth flowed with blood.

The other three stared in horror as Luke sliced off the man's tongue and threw it across the room. He then went over to his cart, grabbed a towel and cleaned himself off and more importantly, he wiped clean his precious knife. Adam saw the feebleness the man was giving off now, stuck there in the fetal position crying and wailing, attempting to form words but couldn't.

"Luke, would you be a dear and sedate the monkey? It seems he may die of blood loss," the doctor said. Luke walked over to the young man, lifting him over his shoulder, and all the while, the young man was whimpering as the blood from his mouth dripped across his bare chest.

Throwing him like a bag of luggage, Luke grabbed a syringe from his cart and began medically attending to his victim. After a few moments, the young man fell silent.

He was unconscious but at least the bleeding had stopped.

"Apologies, Adam," the doctor said sincerely. "It seems that runt has ruined another wise and tantalizing experiment. For this blunder, I'll award you a free pass of sorts. For now, you have ten minutes or so to question the others without the fear of your penalty. I will ensure that the rest of the participants will fall in line tomorrow. That is if you wish to let it lie here for today," the doctor said. Adam looked over at the young man's frail state. He knew the feeling.

The feeling of despair and hopelessness. He wanted to say words of encouragement, to tell him that things would get better if he'd just listen. Yet in his heart of hearts, he knew it wasn't true and remained silent. Looking upon the others, Adam saw their eyes of fear and anguish.

These people's lives were in his hands. Adam looked at the furthest corner of the room and spoke directly to the camera. "I'll just ask my questions and settle it for tomorrow."

The doctor's voice cackled, "Delaying the inevitable, then? Oh, Adam, you have a lot to learn. Shame," the doctor said in condescension.

Adam simply shrugged in a mild indifference.

Adam started with the first female who had caught his eye from the start.

She had fair red hair curling at the sides, her eyes beautifully sharp and bright.

Yet they had a subtlety to them, possibly because their hazel color complemented her red lips, freckles also sprinkled all over her face and body. It didn't detract from any of her beauty; in fact, it would have felt wrong if she hadn't had them in the first place. She was short and a bit stocky but overall, she was stunningly attractive to Adam, nonetheless.

"My name is Adam," he said to the young woman. "Could you tell me your name, and is it possible for you to cross your arms?"

With a little sense of relief, she nodded side to side.

"Adam, my name is Samantha. And no, if we don't keep our arms at our sides and our legs straight, the doctor has told every one of us that he'd kill all of our next of kin. What the hell is going on? Where are we?"

Adam frowned and his eyebrows conjoined in anger.

"So, you three are standing naked like this in order to protect your families? I'm sorry, I just don't get the point at all. He kidnaps you, humiliates you all, and then threatens to kill you and your families if you don't comply?"

Samantha nodded as she wept silently.

"But why?" Adam said in disgust.

"I don't know about the others, but my mother works as one of the board members for Temple Industries, one of the world's largest pharmaceutical companies. Somehow, she and the doctor have ties with one another. I had no idea!"

Tears were streaming down her face. Instinctively, Adam removed his shirt and while looking away, he rolled it a little, placing it over her head before pulling the shirt as far down as possible, hopefully covering her nether regions, which it did.

"Hope this helps?" Adam said still looking away.

"Thank you," she said as she fitted her arms through the shirt, wiping away her tears too.

The male standing next to Samantha rolled his eyes. Feeling his utter contempt, Adam then turned his attention to the male. He was only a few centimeters taller than Adam, yet had a well-built figure and a sharp jawline, his short black hair contrasting with his light-blue eyes.

Had he gone to Adam's high school, he would have been extremely popular for his looks.

"What's your name?" Adam said, annoyed at the male's reaction.

The young man looked at Adam with a piercing gaze of hatred.

"My name is Gale," he said with a nasty scoff.

"Well, Gale. What seems to be the problem?" Adam replied in an almost sarcastic fashion.

"My problem?" Gale questioned. "What do you mean, *my*

problem? I think you're a bit confused. *I* don't have a problem. I actually want to live through this but you're over here flirting, wasting time while you're aware our lives are teetering on the edge of death!

"So, pardon me for dishing out a bit of sound advice but how about you ask as many questions as possible that pertain to the serial killer and make an educated guess?

"Matter of a fact, let me clue you in. Clearly, that idiot with his bloody mouth isn't the killer, and *I'm* definitely not the killer, so you have two choices. It's either this chick, or the one right next to her. So, chop-chop, unless you want all of us dead as well? Do you?"

Adam ignored Gale's response and continued his questioning.

"You don't have any relatives or friends who would have rubbed the doctor the wrong way? Or, you know, trodden on his toes, or something?" Adam asked in sincerity.

"As far as I can tell, no. I was volunteering at a homeless shelter with my uncle. We always do this every Saturday but the night we were closing up the church, two shifty looking dudes clocked one over my uncle's head with a bat. Right out of nowhere!

"The short Asian guy kept beating my uncle till he didn't breathe anymore. The other black guy was holding me back; I couldn't budge an inch. They put a rag on my face and the next thing I knew, I was here." Adam had a theory forming.

It wasn't concrete, but he knew that if what Gale was saying were true, it meant that the doctor possibly was using this church as a source of gathering test subjects.

He didn't want to accuse Gale's uncle outright to his face, but what else could it have been? He nodded in reply and slowly walked toward the other female.

"Hey, as you've already heard, I'm Adam. What's your name?"

"My name is Claire, and my family are just small-town folk. I really can't even think of a reason why I'd be here!" Her cheeks were red and her eyes moist. Her hairstyle was an asymmetrical bob cut and the color a deep black shimmering against the light.

She was beautiful, her slim yet plump figure arousing Adam even more so than Samantha.

Her eyes were emerald green, contrasting with flawless pale skin. Adam could barely keep himself from staring at the rest of her body. A carnal instinct within himself was brewing.

"I had just got off my bus and tried walking over to my apartment. Like Gale, those two men attacked me. So, what are you going to do about this?" Claire replied in a whimsical fashion.

Adam's thoughts were hazy. He never had this many people in a room with him before. Of course, he knew in the past he must have been a socialite but living in this hell hole of a place somewhat regressed his communication skills.

"Listen, I'm just as confused as you all are, and I don't want anyone to die. Yet, I know now that one of you has to die so that no one else has to." Holding the transmitter in his hand, he asked for a confession. "Please, just make this easy for the rest of us. Just tell me which one of you is the serial killer." Gale scoffed at Adam's plea.

He laughed and raised his hands up to his head, clenching his hair.

"I'm going to die here. I'm going to die because of some idiot kid. If you are going to die here because the doctor kidnapped you…" Adam retorted in pity.

Gale looked over to Luke and sneered. "Last I checked, you were the executioner."

Adam could not respond to the clear facts. At the end of the day, he bore some of the responsibility over these people lives. Luke walked over to Adam and outstretched his hand.

Without hesitation, Adam handed the transmitter to Luke.

Tomorrow would be a hell hole from which he knew he couldn't crawl free.

Chapter 8

The next day was as swift as the wind. Adam collected extra pairs of clothes to bring with him just in case. Luke didn't appear to care, and Adam felt he may have an easier time speaking with the other 'patients' if they were fully clothed. As he entered, they stood lined up against the wall at the other end of the room. He could see fresh wounds across their legs and torsos.

Each one looked black and blue, almost as if beaten with a whip. Adam passed out his own spare clothes and understandably, the others were rather quick to put them on.

Samantha and the young man without a tongue were in visible distress.

They perspired a cold sweat of desperation.

Anyone in the room could smell it on them, yet Gale still had fight in his eyes.

Meanwhile, Claire—even though she appeared to be the one beaten the most—simply twiddled with her fingers with an air of confidence not expected from a captive.

All the signs pointed to her.

She had the least compelling story and frankly, she looked too calm for this environment.

Still, rushing toward a rash decision was not the best course of action. Deep within, Adam felt an odd resonance with her, though he would not admit this to himself.

Adam spoke with Gale first to see if there were any holes in his story.

"So, you say you were volunteering at a homeless shelter?" Adam asked.

"Yeah, that's what I said. And what of it?" Gale retorted.

"Just seems odd a guy like you would care about that sort of thing."

"Yeah, and I bet you'd feel that way, wouldn't you?"

"What's that supposed to mean?"

"Just that you're one of those nobodies I'd see all the time in my school. A loser that no one likes or wants."

Adam's teeth gritted and his eyebrows sank into a V shape.

Gale continued, "My uncle made me go, I'll give you that. So, you might be right; I had better things to do than be at that dump, but my uncle was Mr. Right and look where that got him."

Adam didn't like the feeling of his current emotions.

It was a twinge of jealousy and a moderate disdain toward Gale and the ilk of his like.

"I wouldn't go around saying your uncle was Mr. Right, Gale," Adam stated. "Believe me, it won't make you Mr. Popular."

It touched a nerve as Gale walked toward Adam and leaned in close to his face.

Luke crossed his arms watching the spectacle, glancing at the camera as he waited for the doctor's orders, but his voice never gave a hint of direction.

"You wanna run that by me again, twerp?" Gale's tone was one of aggression.

"All I'm saying is it's one thing to be a part of some exchange of currency or medical supplies. It's another to literally provide the stockpile of test subjects," Adam replied with a triumphant smirk. Gale's fist collided with Adam's lower jaw, the impact so strong that it dropped Adam to his knees. He fell to the floor still holding onto the transmitter.

The anger within Adam boiled over. "Who the fuck do you think you are?" Adam screeched. With a flick of the switch marked G, Gale stood motionless, staring at Adam and Luke in awe. A part of Gale thought this was all just a horrible dream. How could this have happened to anyone in reality? Everything was so violent and chaotic here. His last thoughts were of his home, wondering if by some chance this was at all his own fault.

Like a freshly felled tree, Gale's body plunged face first onto the hard laminate floor, twitching every so often like a dead roach. The other male moaned out loud in sheer panic while Samantha shrieked, trembling in fear. Meanwhile, Claire simply yawned, leaning against the wall without a shred of fear. Adam rose to his feet with his palm covering his forehead.

"I just killed someone over a stupid argument, didn't I?" Adam said aloud.

No one responded, almost as if they feared angering Adam any further.

"Hey, I made a mistake. I'm not some monster!" Adam yelled out.

Samantha closed her eyes, looking away.

The male knelt on the floor with a face of defeat.

Claire looked at Adam with a deep fondness and spoke out. "He deserved it, he clocked you in the face and you had the trigger. Don't bite the hand that feeds you, I always say."

She smiled with an almost tantalizing grin.

This was madness and Adam could no longer face his instincts.

Claire must be the killer. Yet why did I hesitate?

Adam turned and looked at the other male.

The one who was alive still… *Why did the doctor spare him?*

Adam had an epiphany. Maybe, just maybe, the serial killer was the loudmouth after all and not once had he conceded to give him his name.

Had the doctor wanted the test to continue, then sparing him would have been the only way. Adam glanced over at the two females with a look of pity.

There was no way either of these two would have been capable of committing those atrocities. With slight hesitation Adam looked at the transmitter.

GTSC, the initials of each patient.

G for Gale, T for Timothy perhaps? S for Samantha, and C for Claire.

Adam looked at the hunched over fellow and sighed. The male flipped upright to his knees, clasping his hands together. No words could form but the loud moaning of pleas and profanities was palpable. He clenched onto Adam's shirt with tears sliding across his withered face.

Closing his eyes, Adam flipped the switch marked as T.

A sharp yelp of desperation ensued, and then silence. A few jerking motions and a small thud to the floor occurred. Finally, there and then, his body was completely still.

Adam looked over at Luke for affirmation.

His dead fisheyes looked back at Adam, and he smiled, shaking his head from side to side. Like a waterfall, Adam's Guilt pounded his very soul to the ground.

His eyes widened and his hand was shaking. Adam had done the unthinkable, having murdered yet another innocent in cold blood. He threw the transmitter away, looking at the man's lifeless body. "Why are you doing this to me!" Adam yelled, clenching his fists.

Both girls stared at one another.

They knew who was innocent, but the problem of the matter was how would he know which one was lying? Adam walked over to Luke in anger and resentment.

"Is this what you do? Help that lunatic like a lap dog!"

Luke's eyes were stone cold; he simply walked over to the transmitter, picked it up and checked if any damage had occurred. Walking toward Adam, he handed it to him.

"Don't do that again," Luke said with a stern yet monotone order.

Adam spat in Luke's face and threw the transmitter across the room.

"Don't you remember what life was like before all of this?" Adam yelled.

Luke cocked his head to the side staring at Adam, looking perplexed.

"It seems you forgot the situation you are in," Luke said broodingly, stepping forward and raising his fist yet in a flash of a second, Adam jumped back a bit, dodging the blow Luke had planned. Of course, this was a war of attrition. Adam kept dodging and weaving.

Luke's fists swiftly and effortlessly missed Adam's body.

Moving back and forth, Adam feinted to run to the left and as Luke reached for Adam, he made a beeline to the cart at the other end of the room, grabbing the knife in his one hand.

"You'll regret this," Luke said plainly without a hint of anger.

Adam bolted toward Luke holding the knife firmly and swung it across Luke's face.

Luke, although very well built, was a bit sluggish in terms of speed.

The knife struck his right cheek just before he could get away. Bleeding, Luke looked toward Adam. "That's my knife. Give it back," he said.

Still pumped full of adrenaline, Adam didn't take heed of Luke's words as he slashed toward him yet again. Luke's hands swiftly grasped Adam by the neck, sacrificing his left shoulder to the knife's onslaught. Adam could feel himself levitating over the ground.

Luke's cold, firm hand was strangling him.

"Continue the test or I'll beat you till the test's time limit is up."

Adam's rage persisted.

He used all the strength in his right arm to bore the knife deeper into Luke's shoulder.

The man-monster bellowed, pain shooting across his whole body, causing his grip to weaken.

Adam swung his legs onto Luke's body, pushing his legs outward with his remaining strength, launching himself a few yards away. The knife lodged into Luke's shoulder, but Adam could hardly care. A little more time spent in Luke's grasp would have been the end of him.

Coughing and disoriented, Adam pushed himself against the wall. Looking up, he could see the damaged pet belonging to the doctor. With no rage and no signs of total discomfort, Luke pulled out the knife from his shoulder and walked toward the cart, cleaning the blade before treating his wounds. The two girls looked upon Adam in awe. Samantha had a look of concern, while Claire, on the other hand, gazed at Luke with a rather odd expression.

A subtle form of anger, perhaps. Adam couldn't quite put his finger on it, but Claire suddenly didn't show any signs of fear or caution.

"Doctor, what would you have me do now?" Luke spoke out.

"This whole thing was botched because of the two males. They simply couldn't adapt to their survival instincts. It seems the females understand the powerlessness of their situation.

"Either way, today was rather productive in another sense, and ten minutes remain on the clock. Just tidy up for now," the doctor replied.

Luke fiddled with the tools in his cart, aligning everything perfectly in a neat order.

He looked at his knife, inspecting for possible flaws as he wiped the blood off with a rag.

"Claire!" Adam called out. "I need to know something. Are you the serial killer?"

Claire's eyes widened as her fingers clenched.

"No, I don't even have a reason for being here!"

"That's the point," Adam said. "Why would the doctor waste his time on some small-town girl?" Samantha showed a sign of relief when Adam questioned Claire.

Claire's face contorted for a moment but then regained her composure. "Some things are better left unsaid, but I'm not the serial killer, Adam."

"Then, how can I trust you if you won't even tell me the truth?"

Claire looked at Adam and smiled. "If I die today, it makes no difference to me. In the end, it'll be your fault when you find out you're wrong, and you will be the one to suffer, not me because I shall be gone. Can you live with that? Think about it. You've already murdered two innocent guys! There will come a time when you are old and sit alone, waiting to be brought to the depths of hell for your mistakes, the ones in which you slaughtered the innocents."

"Tell me the truth," Adam asked perplexed as a whole personality shift had occurred. But the girl was right, and the words sent a vile shudder of white cold down his spine.

Slaughtering the innocents. That was hardly an accolade to take through into old age.

Claire rose an eyebrow and looked at Adam. "Anyway, you have it all sorted out—and you are correct. Claire is the serial killer."

Walking over to the transmitter, Adam grabbed it and held it upright.

"I guess you made this easier for me. Thanks."

Claire looked at Adam with a lustful gaze.

"One more thing," Claire said. "Something you have not even contemplated. *My* name is Samantha. She's Claire. Something else for you to think over, Adam."

With that statement, Adam was back to the drawing board.

"You're not going to believe her, are you? She's lying. My name's Samantha, and she's just trying to confuse you to get off the hook. Please, I don't want to die. Please!"

"Five minutes remaining." The doctor spoke out.

Adam's thoughts swirled through his head.

If I guess wrong, the killer lives, I receive a penalty, and I am now on the doctor's bad side for attacking Luke. Adam's eyebrows raised.

And if I get it wrong, I am slaughtering the innocents, just like she said.

This had been the greatest amount of failure he had dealt with since getting here.

This test wasn't about problem solving whatsoever.

The doctor was testing to see if Adam would kill someone for his own survival. Adam's anger boiled over knowing the doctor had played him like a fiddle.

"Claire!" Adam yelled. "You are the serial killer. Samantha, you're innocent. Am I right?" Samantha nodded her head in agreement as Claire shook her head and laughed.

"No, I'm sorry, but my name is in fact Samantha. She lied from the very beginning, and the only reason I played along was because it was so damn interesting." Claire's eyes sharpened.

"She might not know her real name. You think the doctor plays fair? I may be the killer, but my name is Samantha. You pull that switch that starts with a C, and she will drop dead. Not I."

Adam's resolve was waning. *What if she's telling the truth?*

Studying Samantha, there was no way she'd be the killer. Was that the point though?

Why on earth would someone innocent put themselves this far in harm's way?

Adam's thoughts could only point to one outcome.

No matter what, he was not about to go through another torturous experience again. He looked at Claire; her body was mesmerizing.

Yes, Samantha was definitely attractive in her own right, yet Adam could not help but desire Claire if that was her real name. Adam paused, realizing his thoughts were becoming more and more self-serving. Would he really kill someone based on something so trivial?

Was this why they were naked in the first place?

"Two-minute warning," the doctor said. Adam was sweating just looking at both women.

"I don't know what I should do!" he said.

"My name's Samantha. It's Samantha. Please. Don't kill me!" *Samantha*, or was it Claire, desperately pleaded. Why would I want you to flip my own switch! It literally makes no sense!"

"No, my name is Samantha, and I am in fact the serial killer; you pull that switch with a C, you kill her and that's that. The doctor works in mysterious, cynical ways," *Claire* stated with a grin. *This must be a trick; the doctor always has a twist!*

Adam looked at the transmitter. Samantha screeched in a fit of desperation.

"She is begging you to kill her. Just flip it! My name is Samantha," she shouted.

"One minute remaining, Adam," the doctor spoke out once more.

With no more hesitation, his hand flipped the switch.

In an instant, the redhead's body straightened up and then slapped against the floor. Claire was astonished. "Wow, didn't know you'd trust a serial killer."

She laughed maniacally. "Well, there must have been some reason you picked the name. Were you really trying to kill me, or did you like what I have to offer?" Claire removed her garments and grabbed her breasts, squeezing them tightly and looking at Adam longingly.

Adam sat on the floor, hunched over, defeated.

"I picked Samantha because I thought she was telling the truth. The doctor could have easily made her think her name was Samantha. I don't know; a part of me felt that I'd be making a grave mistake if I took things at face value. The answer was too simple for me," he said.

"That's not true, Adam. You killed her for me," Claire said.

She walked over to the dead girl's body, clenching onto the girl's curly red hair and lifting it a few inches off the ground. She dropped it, making it hit against the hard surface.

"Yep, she is one hundred percent dead," she said in a mocking tone.

"You failed the test, Adam," the doctor said. "However, no penalty will be counted against you and a new test will begin in this very room. So, head back to your quarters."

Adam spoke aloud. "Her blood isn't just on my hands; it's on yours too."

Claire looked over at Adam as she walked to the other end of the room.

"Oh, honey! I have gallons of it and then some." She was laughing.

Adam silently entered his room and headed toward the shower, disgusted with himself.

***

In an undisclosed location within his office, the doctor diligently entered the data according to what had transpired.

"He's falling a lot faster than I anticipated," he said with a menacing grin. "I wonder how long it will take to fully break him in. Only then will his life have meaning."

The sound of tapping keys echoed within the room. "The joy that comes at the expense of others is such an unbelievable high. Controlling the life of an inferior and playing with their fate is my divine right. Once I have compiled all the data I need, I will wreak havoc over the world.

"I will be the Most High and will rule this planet with an iron fist, teetering between the benefit of mankind and my carnal ambitions as they clash every now and again.

"Yet mark my words, the things that I do and the things that I enjoy doing are all for the benefit of mankind. Who is more deserving of the world's throne if not me?

"The savior of mankind, the liberator of morality. When everything is mine for the taking, only then will the inferiors understand. The perfect world for its perfect king."

Adam's eyes opened slowly. Lying underneath the covers of his bed, he contemplated his decision. Perhaps deep down, he had just killed someone for a psychotic freak.

Thinking about Claire, Adam's body slowly drowned in his sweat, feeling it prickling at the back of his neck, rolling down his back and wetting the waistband of his pants.

It was wrong, and he could finally see why Atreus was so hard on himself.

Adam couldn't help feeling restless, wondering if he'd ever see her again.

His thoughts jumbled as his mind tried rationalizing how such a beautiful woman could kill so many innocent people for a cheap thrill. Then there was her habit of posing the dead bodies like mannequins in some grotesque art form. He thought about this, and still couldn't understand.

Imagine doing this to someone, then stepping back to admire your work, adjusting the limbs if necessary. What more could he say? He was smitten by a lunatic and even killed an innocent girl just to let her live based on something so trivial, such as her devilish smile when she proudly admitted to being the killer. Even then, Adam couldn't find in in himself to hate her.

"Get up," Luke said.

Adam tilted his head away from his pillow, staring at Luke for a few moments and then sitting upright on the bed, waiting for what was to come next.

Was Luke going to beat him senseless, perhaps cutting off an appendage or two?

The thought caused Adam to tense up in preparation for another brawl except this time in his worn-out condition, he knew it would be a pointless struggle.

"Take these pills. Doctor's orders." Adam looked at the pills, hedging his bets.

"What's in these? he asked. "What are they for?"

"Does it really matter? Take them or I'll force you to take them," Luke said. "It's your choice. Either take them with a glass of water, or I'll ram them down your throat with something."

Knowing full well this was obviously another test, Adam decided to take the path of least resistance and swallow them with apparent willingness. After a few moments of Luke making sure Adam did in fact swallow the pills, he headed toward his cart at the other end of the room.

"Listen to me very clearly. For the next half hour, I cannot allow you in that bathroom.

"If the doctor pages me and says I have to come back here, I will give you double the dose and slice off your good fingers." Exiting the room, Luke grabbed his cart and walked through the door to the next testing area. Adam microwaved a few meals and grabbed beverages from the fridge, sitting down and devouring all of them. How much more could he take?

How much longer until an opportunity would strike? Adam's thoughts were dead set on escape but every crevice and corner within each room was devoid of any weak spots.

The walls were thick, and the room was in constant surveillance.

He could locate no exploit as he explored his surroundings, pressing his hand against the next testing area's door. He needed to become a nurse—that was the only way of escaping death.

Yet what then?

An eternity of servitude to a deranged scholar? Administering penalties and tests?

Adam sat on the bed, looking at the ceiling, wondering how Atreus had survived so long.

The burden on his shoulders must have been too great to carry any longer in his last days with the doctor. Either he had to become a sick sociopath who enjoyed the suffering of others, or eventually become crushed with guilt and lose his motivation to live.

Adam's eyes narrowed and his eyebrows furled into an expression of rage. Looking at his injured hand, he wondered if it would at least be functional when the time came.

***

A few hours passed as Adam continued to run around the room in circles. *Cardio,* he thought.

If he had been a tad faster, Luke would have never had grasped him. Ten days had passed, making Adam somewhat perplexed. Every day there had been an ordeal specifically catering to him that he had to overcome, and now he felt more like a prisoner than a test subject.

However, he wasn't complaining in the slightest. Luke only came to his room to change his clothes out and stock up on supplies, remaining silent for the duration. Adam continued his physical activities, not only to strengthen himself but also to kill the monotony of the day.

Alas, the time for testing had arrived and Adam felt how fleeting the relative peace had been.

The doctor's voice was loud as always. "Adam, a new test has arrived and if I do say so myself, I believe we will both enjoy it." Adam rolled his eyes at the doctor's snide remark while Luke was dressing Adam's wound again.

"Can you feel anything at all?" Luke asked.

"Not really. Just feels like my fingers are stubs even though I can see the rest of my fingers."

"Give it about a month and you should be able to move your fingers with relative ease," Luke said. Adam could see the desolate eyes that never wavered, seeing that whatever this man was, he wasn't human. Otherwise, how could he be so devoid of emotion and feeling?

Everything was a means to an end for this man.

Frankly, Adam didn't know if Luke even cared about the times he was a patient. Yet was that the point? Did the doctor break him like this or had he come into this world already broken?

Entering the next room, Adam waited for the doctor's instructions.

"Think of this as more of a game than a test. At the start of this game, I will ask you to act upon different choices. For example, if I were to say *stab Claire in the leg or slit her throat,* you must choose between the two." Adam's eyes widened as he heard Claire's name.

He would be playing a deadly game with a serial killer of all things.

"What if I decide not to play your game?"

"Oh, that is rather simple, really. If you refuse, then the more severe the penalty at the end. So, Adam, I suggest that you think carefully about acting upon your insubordinate behavior as of late. Reflect on your actions that brought you to this point. Adapt, Adam! Adapt, I tell you!

"Learn to relish taking these tests and maybe one day, I'll see fit to keep you alive as one of my most favored nurses. Of course, you can always fight against the grain and live like Atreus.

"Although as of recent events, I'm sure you know where that led him."

Adam stayed quiet, simply lost in his thoughts.

Adam couldn't stand the thought of harming someone without cause. *She may be a murdering lunatic but in the end, she's still a young woman to Adam.* From there, his memory spiked, thinking of the good old days where his father took him to the local ice cream shop.

***

His father had been such a champion of male chivalry; Adam could remember him opening doors for women, though his chivalry toward the fairer sex sometimes backfired on the men he encountered. He'd even beaten up a random man for slapping his wife across the face. As the woman fell with tears on her face, Adam's father had bolted toward the assailant, grabbing the gentleman by the shirt collar and punching him over and over in the head till the man's face dripped blood. Unable to stand, the man was dazed and confused.

"What the fuck was that for, asshole!" he'd screamed.

"Next time, try getting a punching bag instead of a wedding ring, kiddo." Adam's father grabbed the woman's hand and lifted her off the floor. "Are you all right, miss?"

She pushed Adam's father aside and held the man who had just beaten her in public in her arms. Crying, she yelled at Adam's father, scolding him profusely as she wiped the blood off her husband's face. They called the police, and Adam's father was gone for a few hours.

The ice cream shop owner sighed as he watched over Adam.

"Here, on the house." Adam looked up at the owner and asked him why his father would do that. The store owner laughed a bit. "You don't go beating on a woman, kid. Your dad's head is screwed on the right way. Good thing too, since it looks like that young buck will think twice before he starts hitting on his woman again."

"Why would she stay with someone like that?"

"Who knows, son? People tend to get attached and once they do, hell, a fella could murder half a city and she'll still defend him." Adam's childlike mindset was too immature to understand the whole ordeal but now his morals were being tested.

Hurting a woman was out of the question.

Adam's mind came back to reality as the door at the other end of the room opened with a fully clothed Claire. She smiled at Adam, waving her hand.

"Hey, stranger. Where have you been?" Claire said.

Adam stayed silent and looked at Claire in disgust.

"Oh, I see," she said with a laugh. "You're still mad about that red-headed chick falling headfirst to the ground. Well, maybe if you didn't press any of the buttons at all, she'd still be alive. Yet you didn't. You're a pussy who didn't want to take the chance of failing and getting a penalty," Claire said. "Maybe, if you actually had some balls, I'd be dead, and she'd still be alive." Adam grit his teeth, staring daggers at Claire.

"Oh, don't be so mad. Maybe you might actually have balls and that's why she died in the first place because you wanted something from me. You don't think I could tell how hard you were trying not to stare at me. Get real. You're not some white knight. You're a guy who wants a girl so bad that you're willing to kill others just to see if you'd ever have a shot with her.

"Admit it, you're a lonely piece of shit who needs the warmth of a woman's touch," Claire said as she caressed herself in odd yet sensual places.

"Shut up!" Adam yelled. Claire's eyebrows raised as she whistled.

"Excuse me, tough guy. I was about to say I was flattered, but now you're going to have to start from square one if you want to get in my pants."

She walked over to Adam and spat on his face, grabbing his lower jaw and looking into his eyes. Adam's anger rose but then settled bit by bit the longer her gaze was upon him.

She stared deep into his eyes as if looking at the very essence of his soul. Adam grabbed Claire's wrist and shoved her hand away from his face.

In the middle of the room were two chairs and a table. Walking over to the table, he sat awaiting the doctor's twisted little game.

Luke entered into the room with his cart and brought it next to the table. He pulled out a foldable chair, sat down, and for whatever reason, began cleaning his precious knife. Sitting directly across from each other, Adam and Claire awaited the doctor's orders.

"The test begins now," said the doctor.

Luke brought out a cart, and upon it was a rectangular box with three color-coded buttons. One red, one blue, and one green. Three monitors slid out from a hidden compartment from the colorless ceiling, looking as though they were melting off the roof.

"Like an icicle, the seasons change," the doctor's voice lightened, giving the details of the experiment, as if he were a waiter naming the Saturday specials. "So, what we have here, Adam, is fairly simple. If you see on screen one, we have a fire department building in New York.

"Nothing special really except today, they have a seminar on fire prevention. The city has decided to highlight this endeavor, creating a charity event for those who have lost everything from a fire. As of late, there have been large volumes of arson and bomb threats."

Adam looked at the screen, perplexed.

"What does this have to do with the test?" The doctor's voice snickered.

In his dim-lit office far separated from the testing area, the doctor cupped his mouth, holding in his dreadful laughter.

"The red goes boom for the boys in red!"

The doctor's eyes squinted tightly as he began cackling loudly like a mad hyena. Claire's eyes rolled as she sat down in the chair, her fingers picking at the uniform's emblem.

"Must be lint, or something," she said calmly to herself.

With Claire's indifference, the doctor's wretched laughter, and Luke's cold watchful glare, Adam couldn't help but sigh somberly. But he remained silent.

"What does the blue button do?" Adam said.

"Ahem!" The doctored straightened himself on his chair and continued, "Yes, well, the blue button is the same as the red except as you see here, there's a hospital building on screen two."

Not much to tell here, just a hospital building filled with the sick and the thankless.

Finally, the third monitor's screen turned on.

"Finally, the green button has the same effect for this location." A house was in view and then all of a sudden, the image was zooming in past a glass window. A red-headed man, woman, and child were sitting at the dinner table, speaking with one another and smiling.

"It's almost poetic, really," the doctor said wickedly. "First you kill the daughter, and now you have front row seats to set aflame her whole family."

"No!" Adam screamed in despair. "Why would you do this?"

Claire whistled again. "Wow, and I thought I had issues."

Adam's guilt was sinking deeper and deeper into the cracks of his already broken soul.

"Do they even know?" Adam replied meekly.

"No, they don't. She was attending college out of state."

The doctor's response was almost chipper. "You have three choices. A building of heroes," he remarked sarcastically. "A building of the sick, or just one measly family who could be spared the pain and misery you have caused them."

"Why is Claire here?" Adam asked.

"Well, you see, Adam. This is your penalty. If you do not choose, I have instructed Claire to pick two facilities instead of one, should you fail to make the choice, of course.

"You have a remarkable pain resilience; seems guilt and fear are more motivating factors."

Adam rose from the chair and the answer was simple.

Samantha's family was the logical choice. Three people or thousands of lives. His hand hovered over the button as he watched the little boy laughing at the table.

"I'm so sorry. I'm so sorry." He could no longer hold back the tears, shaking uncontrollably.

Every inch his hand slowly descended to pass judgment, his whole body rejected it. He could see the mother's loving gaze upon her husband, seeing the worn-out father finally enjoying a meal with his family after a long day of work.

He looked over at the other two screens. Buildings, that's all they were. Maybe they were empty. Maybe they could deal with such a panic. After all, a building seemed as if it could survive a blast better than a small family home.

Maybe, just maybe, the people could be evacuated safely.

Those thoughts came flooding in through his mind. The doctor had tested his will, and now he no longer knew what to do.

On one hand, he could simply kill the family and protect the lives of so many more people. On the other hand, the tragedy that this family would go through was nearly too much for him to bear. He could see their faces, almost smelling the food's aroma escaping from the screen.

They don't deserve this. They don't deserve such a shitty hand in life.

He could spare them; sure, news of their daughter would make them mourn but they still had a son. Right at that momentary thought, the nail in the coffin hit into place.

The boy. He has so much to live for.

The child's innocence looked so pure that the thought of ending his existence felt like an afront to the beauty of humanity itself. Who was he to play judge, jury and executioner for a sick man's game? He should refuse, should tell the freak of a 'doctor' to go to hell. Yet, what would that accomplish? Claire was a notorious serial killer, seeming to be the type to even grasp a sense of enjoyment from it. Refuse to make a choice and more people die.

The hand was no longer his hand. It was a vile putrid thing stained already with the death of three. *More blood will stain these hands.* He could still see their faces every time his eyes closed.

At the rate he was going, they were going to get far dirtier, much more grotesque and viler than he could ever imagine. "The boy doesn't deserve this. Why is this thing still hovering over?" he asked himself. "This thing, this hand so putrid and evil. These are not my hands. I don't recognize them," he said aloud unintentionally.

"You have about two more minutes until I call upon Claire, Adam." The doctor's voice was stern and demanding. Adam's hand halted just a few centimeters above the green button.

What am I waiting for? Do it! Just do it! I have no choice!

The cold sweat down his neck and trailing off his spine sent him into complete hysteria.

Then came a chuckle, small but audible. Then a hiss of lunacy until finally, Adam could do nothing but stand over the button, unable to press it.

He was like a statue stuck in place, laughing and crying, embracing the insanity of it all.

The tears were sliding down with his sweat, his heart also beating as fast as his body was shaking, laughing louder and louder as the seconds kept ticking away.

"I can't do it! I can't fucking do it!" Adam screamed in anger and bloody laughter.

Claire stood up from her chair and slowly walked over to Adam.

His eyes appeared glued to the third screen, hand still stuck above the grim reaper's scythe. Claire touched Adam's face and began wiping the tears off of it.

"You really don't know what position you're in?" Claire said, pitying him. "Better to have three faces stuck in your head than hundreds of them. I would know. I see them all the time."

Nearing the end of the two minutes, she gently guided Adam's hands onto the button.

His eyes closed and his face turned away from the screen.

The intercom screeched as the doctor's voice reverberated in the whole room.

"Why do they always interfere? Luke!" the doctor's voice yelled.

Luke was already standing at attention when the intercom turned on.

"Make him look at the screen!" Adam tried to run to the other end of the room, but Luke had preemptively pounced before the order even came.

The sheer power Luke had seemed unreal. He was a monster of muscle and speed. Feeling someone turning his neck around, a cracking noise gave way when the gloves for hands aligned his face toward the screen. "Open them or I stab," Luke said coldly. Adam could feel the tip of the knife piercing the skin on his back.

"So?"

Utter horror could not even describe this sensation.

Adam's mouth slacked open as he saw the house in flames, watching body parts all over their front yard. The camera zoomed out as more and more neighbors came running outside to see what had transpired. There, in the middle of the clearing of the yard, was the boy dragging himself to his mother's decapitated head. His father appeared to have been closest to the blast, explaining what all the other scattered parts were, those lying on the lawn.

The boy, missing both legs, dragged himself to his mother's head, grasping it. There was no sound, but Adam could see him mouthing out the words.

Mommy, Mommy, Mommy!

By the time the neighbors tried to assist the boy, he had already died from the shock.

Adam's eyes were rolling toward the back of his skull, Luke's fingers pushing against his eyelids. The next form of retreat would have to be his eyes.

Adam wailed and wailed and wailed.

"How could you do this? How could anyone do this? Stop it! Stop it all. Kill me! Kill me! I deserve it. I deserve it!" Luke released him as Adam slumped over to his knees. The doctor's voice came on in the middle of the young man's anguish.

"You do not deserve death just as you do not deserve life. That said, from another perspective, you are a real hero. Sure, Claire had assisted, but I shall give credit where it is due.

"You knew the answer was a numbers game," the doctor said in an almost consoling fashion. "It was either them or this." Right then and there, the doctor ordered Claire to push the red and blue button. Watching Adam's plight, Claire started patting her hands against Adam's back.

"You need to get used to this," she said with what appeared to be a hint of remorse.

"Stop!" Adam broke free from Luke's grip, leaping with all his might and tackling Claire to the floor. "You're not pressing the rest of them!" he screamed. "Forget it."

"Get off of me," she screeched as her nails dug deep into Adam's face.

She scratched and scratched, clawing at his skin. This only spurred Adam forward as he held her right arm in place, biting down hard on her hand. She screamed, crying as well.

"You fucking limp dick, motherfucker!" she raved in complete fury. "I'll kill you! I'll chop off your dick and feed it to the rats of this place!"

Adam, no longer of sound mind, continued thrashing about, releasing his teeth and head-butting Claire in the face. Adam sprang up and attempted to drag her away from the buttons, but as he turned his head to navigate back to the previous room, Luke's fist was already in sight.

First came force, followed by a crunch with pain shooting from his nose to his skull, and finally the darkness's sweet embrace was calling Adam home.

***

Animals behave on an instinctual basis. There is no higher level of thinking bar a few oddities such as dolphins, primates, and of course, humans. The kick of it all is that as far as we can tell, we are the only ones to be truly self-aware. It is a curse, a blind and unending cycle.

To know more is to know less and to know less is to know your own worth.

The driving force of man is no longer to procreate, to hunt, to hide, to gather, and to sleep. No, no, no. Of course not. It could not simply be. Evolution's misguided gift vexes me so. I put the barrel in my mouth yesterday and it tasted sweet. My tongue lavished it the same way it relishes a nightly whore. I wanted it, wanted the taste of death and to feel my brain matter splash like a geyser filled with red honey. It was only for a brief moment.

There is much to be done.

Such vanities should escape me, for as evolution gave us the gift of progress, then I too will reply in kind. Humanity will become calculated. Structured and in order.

An empire of logic, truth, and progress.

I will seek eternity. I will climb the precipice of death itself and laugh. I am meaningless, the same as you are meaningless. Soon, the darkness will come forth to swallow me.

Postponing the inevitable is a fool's errand.

However beautiful it may seem, I must continue my research, must push the boundaries of human consciousness. I will be eternal as eternity has already blessed me with its touch.

Chapter 9

It was new. *These walls have color, a tinge of dark blue.*

A black rotating fan and more furnishings had shown up, also a large desk decorated with sheets of paper and pens. Rising from his new queen-sized bed, Adam walked away from it, feeling the aches all over his body. His neck was stiff, and his hand still throbbed.

Carefully stretching interlocked hands above his head, he tried to straighten out the aches and pain within his torso, slowly arching his back to open up his chest and ribcage.

The bathroom was similar in nature to before. Still plain but slightly bigger.

He had obtained a mirror, an actual mirror.

Initially, it felt like a good idea, but Adam would now have the opportunity to examine his face. *Would I recognize it? If I do recognize it, have I aged? I must have.*

Adam looked at himself for what felt to be his first time. There were bandages on his nose, stained slightly from dripping blood his nostrils expelled. A broken nose, a broken hand, and a sprained neck. He assessed the situation, meticulously feeling around his body.

Oddly enough, the pain within his nose hardly felt like much, and although his hand was still throbbing, he no longer had bandages on it. Just visible stitched flesh where the nubs of his fingers met his palms. Eventually, after he secured himself of anymore possible injuries, he gave time to actually look upon himself. His definitions were sharp and lean.

Short black hair, white yet not pale skin.

Clean shaven and built fairly well. Neither scrawny nor well endowed.

I'm as cookie cutter as it gets, he thought. Straight white teeth. The only thing that made him stand apart were his soft yet bold green eyes. They looked pure and devoid of malice, even though he knew that was far from the truth. Opening the fridge, he found it stocked generously.

He took out two cups of peach-flavored yogurt, three meat, pea, and potato TV dinners, and two bottles of water. Microwaving the meals, he then placed everything on the desk.

Noticing the seat had bolts fastening it to the floor, he slid in between the desk and chair, fitting in comfortably. After gorging himself with the feast he'd 'slaved over' to create, he was lost in his thoughts. *I pushed the button before the two minutes were up. Didn't matter how I did it but that I committed to it,* Adam thought.

"Man of his word, so to speak," Adam scoffed as he looked about the well-appointed room.

Yet out of spite, he told Claire to blow up the rest. So, not exactly a man of his word.

As always, there were only two exits paralleled from one end of the wall to the other. It was surreal; one moment, he'd had a complete breakdown. Yet now, he was at ease.

In fact, I'm more at ease than I have ever been here. Atreus's and Claire's words came to mind. *So, that's it then? Accept the madness, move on or die?* This was frustrating.

"This is sick, I'm sick for even making it this far," he muttered.

The door on his right to the far side of the wall opened. Luke came in quietly and took the dirty clothes out of the bin and replaced the trash can, putting all the disheveled items inside his cart. Pushing the cart over, Luke began unbinding the bandages.

Adam was silent and confused as to why he was not replacing them.

Luke took a flashlight to Adam's eyes, checked his throat, took his pulse, and even checked on his motor skills. Taking a stethoscope, Luke asked Adam to breathe. He noticed his breath was weak and uneven, as if relearning how to breathe effectively.

After Luke cleaned the rest of the room, he spoke to Adam in a monotone fashion.

"The doctor has instructed me to inform you of two things." Adam stood up from his bed and listened with caution. "You and Claire have been in an induced coma for seven weeks."

Adam was surprised how fast it all felt, the transition from a single slumber to seven weeks into the future being a lot to swallow.

"OK, and the other thing?" Adam asked with a tone of annoyance.

"You passed the test and rest assured, we have terminated no other facility. The doctor sends his apologies and admits that the rules were rather ambiguous from the start. He hopes that this will drive you into better success for your upcoming tests.”

Adam simply nodded and walked toward the fridge to grab a can of soda.

***

Pacing back and forth after his routine exercise, Adam was inspecting every nook and cranny of the room, trying to find weak spots or vents that might aid in an emergency escape if the doctor took things too far. He chuckled after that thought. *I guess I have not crossed the line yet, have I? Or rather, does someone keep tugging the line away from me? Were there ever lines not to be crossed to begin with?* Before he could ponder more, the door opened.

It was Claire followed by Luke. The doctor's voice arose abruptly.

“She will be your guest for the next three weeks. The fridge has plentiful stock, and you will have all that you need. The test will begin after Luke leaves the room. There will be no contact or direction for three weeks. Do as you please, and the results will be revealed at the end of the third week.” Luke walked out and closed the door.

Three weeks sealed in a room with a self-proclaimed serial killer. Just wonderful.

“I just want to say that…” Adam's speech was broken as Claire dove onto him as if their struggle from the last test had never ended. She bit down hard on his neck as they both fell to the floor. Using both hands, Adam pried her mouth open before she could draw any blood.

He pushed her off and pleaded with her to stop.

“Those people didn't deserve to die!”

“You put my life on the line, asshole,” Claire screeched as she grabbed onto his arm and kicked him hard in the crotch. Adam reeled back onto the floor as Claire grabbed a nearby towel and rolled it tightly. Just as Adam was getting back on his feet, she wrapped the towel around his neck and dove down to the floor, hoping her weight would put him off balance and break his neck. Luckily, he broke his fall with his hands outreached to the floor.

Claire was still desperately trying to strangle Adam to death.

Adam was at a crossroads, refusing to hurt her but if this struggle were to continue, he may very well lose her life at the hands of another. Regretfully, Adam hoisted Claire off the floor with all his strength. She lost her grip and Adam threw her toward the wall adjacent to the bed.

Adam had thrust himself up onto her, attempting to reason.

"Stop this! Just stop," Adam yelled. "Enough of this! I didn't mean to hurt you before; I just couldn't live with myself if those people had died." Shaking ferociously, Claire stared him dead in the eyes with all the fury a woman scorned could muster.

"Then kill yourself, fuckface, if you can't handle it," she screamed. "I'm going to live and make it out of here. I don't care what I have to do!" Her rage slowly subsided in an uncanny and unnatural way as Adam still held her down, keeping his head held high, preventing her from biting into him. She sighed and then shifted her right leg against Adam's left thigh.

"Do it," she said seductively. Adam's face became flushed and cherry red.

"Just calm down."

"Just shut up and fuck me!" she screamed as loud as her lungs could possibly handle.

Adam's ears were ringing.

Claire roared in anger, "You've been wanting my fuck my insides raw ever since you laid eyes on me. You don't even try to hide it! So go on, do it!"

"I'm not going to do anything to you," Adam said, staring directly in her eyes.

Finally, she relented, and now it was Adam who was gazing into her very soul. He let her go and cautiously stepped back. "I'm sorry that I hurt you," Adam repeated.

Claire rolled her eyes and started massaging her temples.

She walked toward the fridge, grabbed a drink and a bag of chips, then sat at the desk scribbling on the paper, drawing odd symbols and shapes as she ate and drank.

Adam sat on the bed, stunned into a rare silence.

He had to use the restroom but there was no shower curtain or door for that matter. The desk was at the other side of the room, but it was visible for all to see.

Since her back was facing him, he thought this might be his chance.

So, he relieved himself but as he began to use the toilet, Claire stopped her scribbling and turned her head toward Adam's direction.

"You taking a shit?" she asked with a smile. Again, Adam—as red as a tomato—ignored her, face down and finishing his business. Several hours had passed and Adam wanted to sleep.

However, there was only one bed. He grabbed extra towels, placing them on the floor at the farthest corner of the room away from the bed. He walked over to the wall with the only light switch and addressed Claire, saying he was turning the light off.

She nodded and went to the bed.

He attempted to sleep even though in the back of his mind, Adam felt Claire might attack in the night. Yet just as he was crossing over to nothingness, Claire called out, "We can share, you know. I don't have cooties."

Perplexed and flustered, Adam responded, "First of all, I'm pretty sure you do have cooties." He chuckled. "Also, I'm rather more concerned you might try to kill me in my sleep."

He lifted his head to see her sitting upright on the bed.

She laughed gingerly and replied, "You're probably right."

She smirked.

"Which part?"

"Come here and find out," Claire said with a voice of longing.

Adam rolled over on his side facing the wall. "Good night," he said sharply.

"Well, you're no fun."

***

"Why did you kill me?" Samantha said, naked and blood dripping from her empty eye sockets.

"Why did you kill me?" Samantha's father said, nothing but a charred skeleton with empty bleeding eye sockets too. The stench of spilt iron was thick in the air.

"Why did you kill me?" said Samantha's mother, just a head with empty bleeding eye sockets.

"Why did you kill me?" Samantha's little brother said, missing his legs and bleeding from his empty eye sockets. Samantha and her family all were standing before Adam, next to each other from left to right. Starting with the boy, then the girl, then the mother and then the father.

They just stood there, looking upon him against a backdrop of complete darkness.

He stood there motionless, mouth agape in utter fright.

The words wouldn't come out. Slowly, one by one, the figures dispersed into the darkness except for Samantha. She was still there.

She walked over and began undressing him. Adam, still frozen in fear, could do nothing. Samantha then laid him onto the floor and proceeded to use him.

"No! No! No!" Adam awoke in a cold sweat, but confused and dazed, he felt a powerful force pushing down upon him, preventing him from moving much until he realized what exactly was happening. She pushed him down with those delicate but strong hands.

Galloping on him over and over again, Adam couldn't make her stop.

He didn't want her to stop. Yet he pleaded with her to stop. "Get off me!" Adam said with a weak moan. Claire immediately pressed her hands on his mouth.

"Shut the fuck up. I'm almost there."

Adam's mind couldn't process such fear and euphoria.

He was tired and no longer cared, so he relinquished himself to her, allowing her to have her way with him. Finally, she yelled with sweet bliss calling out his name as they both climaxed.

She shared a single deep and wet kiss. Then it was over.

She stood and walked back over to the other corner of the room and lay back in the bed, her lower half exposed. Adam's heart was pounding but it was the first time that it pounded for pleasure and not fear. Both slept soundly that night afterward.

All that transpired was in plain view of the doctor's eyes behind the screen. He lay in his chair like a pleasured whore, pants unbuckled, and his hands sullied with a white substance.

"What was that about?" Adam said.

Sitting at the desk, Claire took a bite of a sandwich and looked up from the drawing she was working on intently. "It was a necessary chore," she said nonchalantly.

"A necessary chore?" Adam asked, slightly offended. "Thought it meant more than that?"

"Listen, I got what I wanted, and you look like you got what you needed. Let's leave it at that, eh?" For the first time, Adam felt used and exposed.

An odd but amusing sensation, he thought later in the day.

Adam noticed within a drawer of the desk Claire was using was a stack of books.

"Hey, you noticed these?" Adam questioned.

"No. Actually, I was too busy trying to kill you." She smiled. Adam sifted through the volumes and found they were all children's books.

A novel about a talking cat, a picture book filled with zoo animals, and a book about making friends. It wasn't exactly prime entertainment, but the only alternative was drawing.

Something told Adam that Claire wasn't really big into sharing.

***

Unbeknownst to them, Adam and Claire had been living in the same room for about three days. They were beginning to stink but neither Adam nor Claire made the first move to use the shower. Adam was reading intently a book about making friends, the title being, 'It's OK to have friends.' The book's audience were little children.

However, to Adam, this was groundbreaking information, learning about making compromises, sharing one's feelings, and keeping secrets—a novelty to those who had never seen or at least couldn't remember the outside world very clearly. His nose was twitching from the smell: enough was enough. Removing his clothing, Adam walked to the shower and under the warm flow of water, started lathering with soap. Then the footsteps became audible.

Adam pretended to not notice but shortly after, Claire's body pressed against his back.

Both parties were fully exposed and this time, with the lights beaming from the ceiling above.

"Hey, what are you doing? I won't be long, then you can have the shower to yourself," Adam said. Claire shifted to the front of him as the water cascaded across their wet bodies.

She kissed him gently, her piercing eyes fixed on his.

She latched onto *it* with a firm grip and his face was no longer sheepish.

"Is this another one of your 'necessary' chores?" Adam said sternly.

She let go and looked at him, clearly dropping her seductive facade. "You don't get it, do you?" Claire said in anger. "At any moment, we might die. And at any time, we could be sent into private cells, staring at a white wall with nothing but torture on the horizon.

"I'm treating these three weeks as a vacation. I don't care if he's watching or trying to get us to pass this test. I'm not going to just curl up into the fetal position and be in fear."

Adam looked at her wet pale skin, still able to smell the faint amount of sweat before she entered the shower. It aroused him; in fact, everything about her aroused him.

Skin as pale as the moon, hair as black as the darkness he had embraced many times over by death's door. Her breasts, firm and supple, contrasted with the pink hue of their tips.

He grabbed her plump rear and shifted her across to the end of the wall.

It was his turn this time and he had to make sure she'd pay tenfold for her past transgressions. Her cries of utter euphoria reverberated against the room's walls.

***

Adam and Claire became synergistic in nature after two weeks forced together in the room. She would sketch while he would read. She would eat when he would eat. He would wash when she would wash. They shared the same bed after the first week, fulfilling their carnal desires frequently. Eventually, Adam became enamored with Claire, so much so, he even contemplated telling her how he felt. It was always important to share one's likes and dislikes, *ice breakers* as they called them. However, he couldn't remember what exactly he liked.

Yet upon these thoughts, he regained a memory.

He could see a stadium, one that he entered, and people were cheering. Music played and people rejoiced. He sat down with friends from school and saw men the size of gladiators ramming into each other at godlike speeds, all chasing a brown oval-shaped ball.

"Football! I like football!"

Claire was enjoying a small cake while Adam spoke out loud suddenly.

"Good for you, Jarhead," Claire said, rolling her eyes.

"Well, what do you like?" Adam asked intently. "Memories are slowly coming back to me. Are you getting the same?"

She shrugged. "Killing men, I guess?" Adam's mind finally became grounded in reality.

"You're a serial killer," Adam said disappointingly.

"Yes, as I've said, even *shown* you several times, stupid," Claire said with a sarcastic grin.

"So why haven't you killed me yet then? Why am I so different?" Adam asked.

"You don't fit the criteria; in fact, I would have killed you earlier, but you still wouldn't fit."

"Still wouldn't fit?" Adam asked. Claire scratched her head and spoke clearly.

"I kill rapists and pedophiles," she said plainly. "Those who inflict damage on the vulnerable. And I don't think you fit in that category, so you're safe."

Adam was confused but understood.

"But how would you know if they were?"

"That's easy. I was a prison, slash, grief counselor. Men who admitted to me what they'd done were never in short supply. Some women got into the mix, mainly the ones trying to bat for them, trying to defend their actions in one way or another. In my eyes, they are equally responsible, all just as culpable."

Adam scratched his head and tried his best to be appalled by her behavior. Yet he really couldn't. In a sense, he'd done much worse to those less deserving anyways.

"Well, didn't you rape me that first night?"

"I did, and it felt great. Were you traumatized?" Claire questioned with a smirk.

Adam shrugged.

"Do you like killing people? Do you get satisfaction from it?"

Claire walked away without a word, grabbed a snack and fell silent for a time.

Adam didn't know what to do, so he lay in the bed and closed his eyes.

Awoken abruptly, Adam could hear Claire next to him in the darkness.

Her cries of anguish, fear, and turmoil penetrated his very soul. In the darkness, he cradled her, comforting this confused female lying next to him. One killer comforting another.

In that very darkness, he felt her warmth as she felt his. She stopped her cries, managing to relax once more, snuggling into Adam. As they both slept, their kinship grew, a newfound feeling blossoming into both their hearts.

***

The third and final week was near its end and Claire's demeanor changed.

She grew distant, cold even. Adam attempted to speak with her, and she would simply nod or sway her head. Communication was at its lowest and Adam could not help but feel at fault.

He grabbed her shoulder as she walked away from her desk.

"Was it something I said?" Claire's eyes winced and relented into a crescendo of tears.

"Don't look at me! Don't look at me with those eyes!" She was shaking. Adam grasped her firmly in an attempt to console her. She responded in kind, her arms cradling his neck tenderly across his shoulders. Then it was all too clear. As he held her tightly in his arms and she wailed against his chest, a sharp pang of pain struck right at the base of his neck.

The red liquid slowly flowed downward into his shirt collar. Time stood still and he could see her eyes filled with regret and indecision, the knife sticking in the position of salute.

If it were plunged past the outer layers of his skin tissue, the curtains would finally close, ending his suffering and wiping away the madness through which he had been living.

For a moment, there was just silence. Claire's doe-like eyes wept and wept as her lips trembled. In contrast, her grip on the knife and its precision was tried and true.

One move, one false step and she was prepared to plunge the dagger deep within his neck, prepared to end him for her gain. Claire looked at Adam and spoke.

"I want to hate you, I really do. You never let me hate you. You give me nothing but grief. I told you I was a killer. I told you to kill me. Yet you wouldn't, would you? Because you men are all the same. You think about what pleases the eye. But what about the soul?" Claire paused. "Mine is as dirty as they come. You wanna know why I kill?"

Adam, nearly as calm as he had ever been, spoke slowly. "I want to know if you enjoyed it."

She bit her lip till her shiny white teeth were tainted with red.

"I loved every minute of it. I get to take it back. Take back what belongs to me."

"So where does this leave us?" She laughed sadly and without mirth.

"I don't know but if you try to get away, I'll do it. I swear, I'll fucking shove this thing into you. I'll do it!" Adam's eyes became soft and reclusive for a moment.

He stared at the floor, dropping the eye contact she oh-so desired.

"You hate me, don't you?" Adam looked up and regained their connection.

"I don't think I could ever really hate you. These past few weeks have been the best of my life. I can't remember anything else from my past and the only thing that I remember before this was blood and violence. I'm content."

Her face contorted in anger and confusion.

"What the hell is wrong with you? You don't wanna live? You don't want to get the hell out of here and see the world for what it is?"

"Give me a break! You're so damn pathetic!" she said.

Adam's eyes faltered slightly, the bridges of his lower eyelids welling with water but not enough to call them tears.

"I have lost the person I was. I don't remember anything but pieces of a lost history, nothing at all. The life of someone else… Well, he's dead and when he died, I was born into this hellhole.

"So, honestly, no, I'd be OK with death," Adam said. "I have no life outside these walls, I have no idea how long I've even been here and to top it off, I don't think it'll end anytime soon."

Claire's anger flushed away and her once steady hand set off shaking ever so slightly.

"This isn't right!" she spat out. "He gets to play God with our lives! He knew this would fucking happen; he knew it!" Adam, unconcerned with her speech, drew her into him even closer. "Of all the people that I thought would kill me, you're definitely the nicest."

"It's OK, I don't want to be here anymore unless it's with you."

His head slowly descended close to hers until both their foreheads conjoined as if into one.

All the while, the dagger followed closely.

"I've been reading, reading about how people need one another. How making friends can relive some of the pain this world has to offer. Yet this is different; you're *not* my friend."

"What? Not at all?" Claire said in disappointment.

"You mean so much more to me than that," Adam said. Their eyes locked into position.

He closed his, tenderly kissing her gentle lips. As sweet and tender as his lips were to Claire, she could not get rid of the bitterness of their intimacy. So bitter in fact, that no amount of fear and pain could topple the feeling this young man's death would cause her.

So, she relented. The dagger fell to the floor and the thralls of passion overtook them.

Shortly after their moment of bliss, they gathered their clothes and collected themselves. They laughed, trading Claire's silence with nonstop communication.

She regaled him of her life in high school, her friends back home. Her volleyball team, her graduation, her college days and finally, how she went to prison.

"It wasn't so bad," she said with a chuckle. "I still had a doctorate in psychology and most of the women I treated were in there with me. I went from working with the system to being a part of the system." She laughed gingerly at the irony of it all.

Listening intently this whole time, Adam decided to speak.

"Well, a psychologist is supposed to know things about people that they might not know about themselves. What is there to say about me?"

Claire looked upon Adam with a soft smile and responded.

"Well, I'm a firm believer in nature versus nurture, in that nurture is the main factor and nature just an added bonus or hindrance. I believe you naturally are a very warm and kind person," she said, looking at Adam dotingly. "That being said, I can't really tell much about the nurture part of you. You don't remember who you used to be, and apart from basic communication, your social skills are atrocious. Everything about you is at face value, honest and easily read. I can tell when you're upset, happy, frustrated, and even horny. A person's personality is shaped by their experience. Take that away and all you have is a blank canvas."

Adam smiled. "So I guess you get to paint my new memories?"

Claire's eyes faltered somewhat. "Yes, I guess no matter what, I'll always be a part of you from now on." A sad soft smile was on Claire's face as Adam used one hand and lifted her chin.

"Always," Adam said with a warm open smile, his eyes free of judgment, free of resentment, and free of authority. The door from the right side of the room opened.

Luke brought in the cart and strolled it toward them.

Adam focused on Luke. "What is it? Time's up?" Adam asked. "What's the next test and what do we have to do?" He seemed frustrated that the moment had to receive an interruption by this soulless machine with flesh. Claire not once dropped her gaze off of Adam when Luke entered. Instead, she placed both hands on his face, trying to steer away his attention.

Adam could feel her pulling him closer to her and for a moment, resisted.

He relaxed when Luke simply ignored him and waited.

Claire looked into Adam's soul and Adam looked into Claire's.

Rubbing his face gently with her left hand, Claire kissed Adam.

"I love you, Claire," Adam responded, not realizing he must have known the words to his feelings this whole time, a love borne between two lost spirits the world had thrown into the pits of despair. Two spirits tainted by the cosmos and its ever-hateful roll of the dice for man's fate.

Claire laughed with tears on her face and a bitter smile. "And I love you!" she said with a profound power, as if it was a deceleration of defiance, freedom, and truth.

A loud crack broke this scene of love and jubilee. There it was as always.

It never left and never held back. The madness came, and it came with a vengeance, so hard in fact, that it ripped apart Adam's very core. His mouth was agape, his eyes bulging, his face as red as the blood in his veins. A torrential roar of unquantifiable magnitude.

Adam clutched at Claire's body, lifting her to his chest as her head dangled backward.

"No, no, no, no, no, no!" Adam repeated ritualistically, screaming and hollering like the ravings of a madman. Lifting Claire's head with his other hand, he tenderly wiped the blood from the right side of her temple, parting the hair covering her face and latching onto her with unbridled rage and anguish. "I love you!" he screamed. "I love you!"

He was crying onto her chest like a baby who has just found his mother in a crowd again.

His mourning lasted for hours, and the hours grew into days.

When his eyes no longer produced tears, he closed them.

When his bleeding throat could no longer curse at the world, he silenced. When his body could no longer contort and writhe like a wild beast, he lay still.

Luke left the room as quickly as he had entered it, putting away the Berretta M9 he had just fired at Claire's head at point-blank range. He quietly wiped some of the blood splatter off the floor and walls with a rag and spray, strolling away with the cart, closing the door behind him as though he had just swatted a fly or cleaned up some dog shit.

Adam's tirade began.

Slumping over and defeated, he held Claire's lifeless body in his arms, cradling her, rocking back and forth. Every so often, he kissed her cold dead lips as if she were ill.

"Everything is going to be OK. So what if you have a hole in your head? It's OK, I still love you," Adam murmured in the corner of the room. "You'll get better soon and then we can talk again, just you and me. You and me," he stated rhythmically for several hours after.

He no longer ate, no longer showered, and he no longer had the will to keep his eyes open. The darkness called out to him and swallowed him whole except as he faded into its embrace, he could see Claire calling out to him devoid of any sound. Her hand was reaching for him as if to pull him away from the darkness. Yet the darkness was peace, it was quiet, and warm.

Within the backdrop of absolute nothingness, tendrils formed, sprawling out like a nest of snakes hunting the same creature. They enveloped his body, pulling him deeper into its bosom.

For a moment, he struggled, trying to reach for Claire's hands.

A light he had never seen before appeared behind her, sparkling and glistening, piercing the darkness like a sword. The tendrils relinquished their hold, and, in a moment, Claire's hands met his and they embraced. No words tainted the air, no words audible. But they knew.

They knew their brief encounter was spurred on by their environment, that these emotions and feelings may have faded over time had they met in a different life.

They both thought *so what,* in this pitch-black darkness with the single ray of light. Here they were, fueled by their love and affection. It didn't matter to them how long they'd known each other but rather that these three weeks they'd spent together were the best times of their miserable lives. He could feel her pull away and desperately tried to hold on.

Just a few more minutes, he thought as he counted each second, staring into her beautiful face. She smiled as her mouth expressed the words, *I love you*.

Then she vanished, the light gone and his love with it. The tendrils reformed and pulled him gently back down. Down, down, down, into the pits of nothingness.

Chapter 10

"Oh, Adam. It's time for your results to be shared!" the doctor's voice called out with the gratified malice. Adam awoke from the bed and took in his surroundings.

A new room, two doors on opposing sides and one door in between the two in its respective side. He walked toward the single door because this one actually had a handle.

Beyond the door was a bathroom filled with all the accoutrements he would need to clean himself. He moved outward to see a dresser filled with multiples of his same attire.

He had a full-sized fridge, a bigger desk with a chair, a small couch facing his bed in the middle of the room, and finally, a monitor flush with the wall itself right above his bed.

"Well, do you like it?" the doctor's voice inquired. "My God, you have earned it, Adam! I'm astonished by these results!"

"Results!" Adam replied with an equal and almost evil-like quality. "How does making me suffer provide results?" Adam spoke, gritting his teeth.

The doctor's voice fell silent, and the monitor turned on.

"It's provided many results to which frankly, you are not privy, you swine!"

On the monitor was a face that paired with that wretched voice.

"Well, Adam. It's finally time we see each other face to face, wouldn't you think?" the doctor replied coldly. Adam's expression contorted into a cold-blooded glare.

His hate and revulsion grew all the while as his innermost thoughts were filling with depraved and decrepit images of glorified vengeance.

He could picture it, could almost taste the doctor's flesh and blood in his mouth, biting down and gnawing at the doctor's shriveled and weathered neck, wishing to slash and pummel the doctor's plain face with his own two hands and to rip the remains of the doctor's hair at the sides of an otherwise bald scalp down the middle. An old bald-headed white man.

Hardly any memorable features except for dull green eyes.

Nothing like Claire's glimmering emerald ones.

He wanted to pull away his prim white lab coat and strangle him till the fabric embedded into his skin. The doctor could see it as well. He could see the images oh so clearly.

He could see Adam's innermost thoughts, couldn't help but lick his lips, massaging the armrests on his chair on which he casually rested.

A slight bulge in his pants formed underneath the camera lens's view.

"You hate me that much?" the doctor asked. Adam's eyes mellowed and relaxed.

"No, I don't hate you, doctor, and I apologize if I somehow conveyed that in any way."

Adam grit his teeth and receded his malice, pulling it back as if he were trying to cage a mad dog that was attempting to pull away from its master.

"I like the room; it definitely shows how much you care, and I am very thankful for it." Adam knew there was no point in wasted anger, so he lied through his teeth in an effort to make progress. Bit by bit, he would gain the doctor's trust and bit by bit, he would conceal his emotions until the moment was right, just right enough for him to strike.

The doctor's expression couldn't have been more enthused.

He looked like a cat toying with its prey, relishing the moment before it ate its meal.

"So, a few explanations are in order. You see, Claire, although a wonderful patient, did not really exemplify what this facility was trying to accomplish. So very obedient, so focused on survival, she barely gave any hint of hesitation."

The doctor's eyes looked toward the ceiling, massaging his temples with his right thumb and index finger. "We need raw emotion. We need passion, and we need…"

The doctor paused for a moment, searching for the best word to describe it. "We need patients to struggle," he said with a nasty grin, even though his teeth were perfectly aligned and pearly white. "Tragedy really. She came here already matured. Too well put together, a beautiful canvas of blood and hatred. You could agree that the fire within her was tremendously bright, dazzling even," the doctor said almost regretfully.

Adam's rage manifested its own will and he nearly lashed out at the monitor, withdrawing it even deeper into his subconscious. *Now is not the time. Hold it,* Adam pleaded to himself.

Hold it in and take it. Don't give him the satisfaction, he thought.

The doctor, almost impressed at Adam's calm demeanor, now felt challenged. He wanted to see Adam's rage. To see those eyes of hatred peer into his soul.

"What a shame really. Her mother was a whore of the night, you see. She paraded herself around like a used sponge until finally, she met a man just as filthy as her.

"Claire, born out of wedlock, was destined to have such a difficult life. Malnourished and alone, she had resorted to stealing and violence for survival," the doctor said in a poetic fashion.

"They all lived in a one-bedroom apartment in the dung heap of a town, her mother lying on her couch as she casually overdosed on methamphetamine, and all in the same moment as her own biological father violated her in every which way possible on her fifteenth birthday."

The doctor's voice was growing louder as if aiming to reach a crescendo.

"Then, when it was over, he would beat her savagely, blaming her for the atrocity he had just committed. She cried and begged for mercy, but it never came, of course."

The doctor rose from his chair and leaned in closer to the camera. "It happened again and again and again in an endless cycle of pain and debauchery!" the doctor yelled.

Adam's will was waning but continued to be steadfast.

The doctor readjusted himself.

"Eventually, the proper authorities of her school caught wind and set her up for adoption. Shortly after, her father killed her mother, and he fell in suit a week later due to alcohol poisoning. The bastard died peacefully in his sleep. Thank fuck for that."

The doctor chuckled.

"There is no justice in this world, Adam. The world just is, and that is all it ever will be. Don't let anyone tell you anything different. The world is a cesspit of unfairness and injustice."

It made Adam's sensibilities burn to hear the man speak like this;

he, the so-called doctor, was a cesspool of injustice too, all on his own! So, how could he say the world was so bad?

The doctor pondered for a moment and looked at Adam almost in a shy manner.

"Unless you could help me change that?"

Adam was silent and deep in thought. "Now all the pieces were there. Her life fell forfeit from the start. She never had a chance to begin with. So, she decided to create her own justice."

"So why did she have to die?" Adam said.

The doctor rolled his eyes.

"I needed her choices to be difficult. I needed hesitation and self-doubt. You helped facilitate those, Adam. My precious Adam, you were her vice, her weak link, so to speak. I gave her these instructions." The doctor recited his demands in order. "First, she was to stay with you for three weeks in your quarters. Second, she was given a dagger and I told her to keep it hidden and never reveal it until the final day. Finally, I instructed her in no uncertain terms to kill you on that final day. Luke waited patiently until the time was up, even taking his time, letting her final words reach you, so to speak. I was a tad perturbed but Luke is hardly ever an issue.

"He deserves some wiggle room, wouldn't you agree?"

Adam had gathered it was something along those lines.

"So, she died for me because I was the only one who cared. You made her struggle by giving me up to her and leaving my fate in her hands?" Adam spoke in a monotone fashion.

The doctor's hands clapped rapidly.

"Bravo, my dear boy. Bravo. Then she knew true struggle! It's easy to kill those you despise!"

The doctor was filling with passion, imbuing his words with it.

"But to kill those we perceive are innocent! To kill those who love us! To end the lives of others free of blame!" The doctor's voice was louder than ever and filled with incredible fervor.

"Now she knew the cost! Now the power of the human psyche had laid its force, destroying the fabric of her nature, the very nature of her survival, Adam! She evolved and bloomed into a fine woman, a woman beyond her very sense of self-preservation!"

The doctor's head had risen at a full one eighty.

His arms spread forth like wings and his eyes were nearly bulging out of the skull.

"For years, she toiled like a useless chimp but then finally, she accepted my gift with open arms!" The doctor wailed in madness and hysteria, drooling from his mouth as the bulge in his pants grew bigger and harder. Adam could not believe what he was hearing.

This man was mad; he had always known it always to be true, but he had not taken into account quite *how* mad this man truly was.

"So, what's next?" Adam asked nonchalantly.

"Ahem." The doctor composed himself and smiled gingerly. "More tests, of course."

The door closed behind Adam as he walked into the next room.

This one was damp with a chill in the air, but it was nevertheless a considerable size at about the length of half a football field. Looking at his feet, Adam realized he was on a platform, connected to a narrow footbridge formed skillfully out of metal.

Underneath, the shimmer of open water, from one end of the room to the other.

Adam looked around in amazement. He had never seen such a large body of water in his life. He quickly recanted that thought and knew that deep within himself, he must have been able to remember the smell of chlorine from a public pool he would visit frequently as a child.

The memories were not there but his body could never forget the countless hours of breaststrokes and cannonballs, and even of trying to swim the length of the pool underwater.

As he continued on, the bridge shifted abruptly with a loud thud from below his feet. He nearly fell off the railing by his side but was able to grab a firm hold of it in the nick of time.

"Careful there, little one. You have friends below, and we wouldn't want them to meet you just yet before you're given instructions!" the doctor's voice bellowed over the intercom.

It was so loud, in fact, that Adam clasped his ears in annoyance.

After a few seconds, Adam asked, "So, what do you want me to do now?"

The doctor's voice became firm yet shrill.

"Farther down into the middle of the bridge, there is a hole for you to enter the water below. You'll easily recognize it. From there, you will swim down to the very bottom of the tank and grab the key tied off to a weight. Once you have it, you must swim to each corner of the tank, unlocking each mini chest containing a three-dimensional shape. You need all four to proceed to the next room." Adam looked toward the clear blue water.

How sick a game the doctor had in store for him now.

There were massive, huge beasts of the deep; while he couldn't tell what they were, the fear and tension ran down his spine. These were great white sharks of a peculiar design. Deformed and misshapen, their features were unlike any beast concocted from the ocean's depths.

No, Mother Nature was not so perverse and volatile.

The vast creatures' fleshy fins forked into two, also twisting at their ends while their rounded eyes were gray, surely devoid of any capability of sight. A large gash just below each of their bellies seemed to have been sewn shut, and ahead of their dorsal fins perched small antennas permanently latched onto their skulls. They were as large as a regular automotive vehicle with mouths that could easily swallow three grown men whole.

There were four in total, swimming in an almost methodical sequence.

"That's all there is to it," the doctor stated gleefully.

Adam walked around the hole and jolted toward the other side of the humongous tank.

As he sprinted, he could see all four dorsal fins pop out of the water in mere moments, gliding across the water's surface and gaining in speed as they spearheaded toward Adam.

The clanking and pounding his feet made sent vibrations to the beasts, as if the dinner bell were ringing. Finally, out of breath and in sheer panic, Adam desperately looked for a handle.

He was pounding on the door.

"I can't do this! This is impossible! Let me out. I failed, OK. I failed!" Adam yelled in defeat. The intercom screeched and a deep sinister laughter echoed all across the room.

"You fail, you die! These doors will never open, Adam. No more options left, you see? Either you will you pass this test, or you can starve to death for all I care!"

The sharks stopped in sequence now, hovering around Adam, circling in pairs on each side of the bridge. Adam could see that hollowed-out patches lay right in the middle of the door.

A sphere, a cube, a tetrahedron, and an octahedron.

Grazing the hollowed-out edges, his fingers started to tremble. He noticed the steel door, bolted shut with a mechanism that appeared to lift the door open should the correct shapes find their places in their allotted sections, similar to the children's game in which wooden blocks have to slot into the right-shaped holes. He tiptoed slowly to the other end of the room.

At first, the sharks followed, but slower and slower each time he took a careful step.

Take it easy, Adam. The fewer vibrations the better, he thought.

Stirring the water was a death sentence. Though the other door was not as heavily reinforced, it was impossible to break through. After hours of banging against the door, pulling at its handle and begging the doctor to open up for him, he accepted his fate.

The sharks, having caught wind of his tantrum, again circled in pairs around him.

He immediately stopped all of his motion and waited.

After about three hours, they returned to their respective corners and Adam's breathing relaxed. His throat was sore from all his pleading and the white-cold fear made his legs weak to a point he could barely stand. So, he did not try to. Instead, he curled up his weakened form at the end of the door and slept in the cold, bright room, his eyes jolting wide awake every so often.

Eventually, his consciousness faded and accepted the darkness once more, all the while those abominations still circled in the motionless and stagnant waters.

Falling, the sensation crossed his mind. No, it wasn't quite that.

More like sinking slowly to the bottom of the endless abyss that was the darkness.

He opened his eyes to the backdrop of nothingness once more.

Things had changed again. Now, it wasn't warm but cold. He couldn't breathe since every time he gasped for air, there was nothing. No solids, liquids or gas.

He felt as if enveloped in oil, his hair and clothes unable to provide any friction as he sank deeper and deeper into the darkness. It was almost as if he found himself in the depths of a vile polluted ocean away from the sun's beautiful rays of hope.

His eyes adjusted somewhat.

And there it was now, lying still and motionless, staring into Adam's eyes. One of the beasts from the tank, breathing heavily like a deranged bulldog, slobbering and oozing a foul and slimy odor from its mouth, the massive rigid maw showing rows and rows of sharp decaying teeth.

As it exhaled, its eyes mimicked a chameleon's, moving in varying directions opposite from one another, searching with a desperate sight it no longer even possessed.

The rancid great gash below its belly tore apart as ingested bodies came crawling out, hands pushing outwards and breaking apart the stitches, fingers twisting and writhing, entangling themselves in the bloody mass of weakened stitches, feeling their way free.

Like a geyser, all the flesh dropped and let out a loud *ker-thunk* as they hit the bottomless floor. Here were bodies with missing limbs and skin, some with their heads still intact, others just a torso with vaguely attached legs. Yet they all had the same bile and acid dripping from them.

It was impossible to identify whether they belonged to a man or woman. It didn't really matter, of course, anyway; these were so mutilated that there couldn't possibly be any distinction.

They all sprawled and crawled out like worms retreating into the soil, slithering and sliming about and fading into the darkness.

All but one body, surprisingly intact and exhibiting some masculine features.

As it moved closer to Adam, the shark swam away as if to search for all of the food that had escaped it, dripping all kinds of fluids and leaving behind a visceral train into the sheet of black.

Adam tried swimming upward but to no avail, and he could feel the lack of oxygen affecting him tremendously. The man-like creature reached out and grabbed Adam's face as he flailed wildly. Looking away from its putrid visage, Adam could hear a familiar voice.

"Adam, you got to get used to it," the creature whispered, holding onto his face. "Do it for me!" it screamed, dragging Adam's head into forceful eye contact.

"Atreus?" Adam gasped in confusion, then his eyes opened as he called out to Atreus once more. The dream was gone and reality set in.

"I either die slowly, or die quickly," he whispered. "Either way, I die."

He pondered on the pain and agony the teeth would cause as they set about ripping into every muscle fiber in his body. *Maybe the shock will kill me before the pain arrives.*

Sad, really, he thought as a small chuckle escaped on his breath, then slowly increased in decibels as Adam's lunacy came creeping out, etching at the sides of his skull, tearing at his hair and skin while he laughed in pain and sorrow.

"Shit or bust!"

Silence.

He stood up and walked to the middle of the bridge where he quietly dove headfirst into the clear blue water. The water was cold there but not unbearable.

He ignored all his surroundings, simply focusing on the key floating at the bottom of the tank just as the doctor explained. The weight itself lay fastened firmly to the key; he couldn't quite get it off without forceful tugging. Completely resigning himself to his heinous fate, he acted as if he had no care in the world. He would either die in the tank or live to see hell once more. Would it make a difference either way? To live like this was to die. And to die was freedom.

It was the way of things, and there was no changing it.

Finally making headway, the strap released the key.

Adam had it grasped in his hand, dropping the weight without a second thought. A small thud hit the bottom of the tank and in an instant, as if he had a sixth sense, Adam looked all around.

The beasts had heard the *dinner bell* and all four maws opened wide as they dived toward him at the bottom. With all his might, he pushed off from the bottom and toward the bridge at the surface. Accepting fate? Dying quickly? Allowing monsters to tear him apart?

These thoughts vanished as Adam's survival instincts kicked in, flooding him with adrenaline and a will to live unlike any he had known before.

They gained on him, closer and closer, inch by inch but by sheer luck, he pushed his body onto the bridge through its opening and lay on his back, coughing and hacking away at the vile water that was entering his lungs. Bang! A large jolting force hit the bridge. *Bang! Bang! Bang!*

Three other tackles at the bridge nearly knocked Adam back into the water along with the key firmly latching onto his dead man's grip.

He crawled slowly toward the door at the farthest corners away from the door with its hollowed-out shapes.

Adam's blood rushed toward his throbbing head and every inch of his muscles wanted to lock into place. It took every ounce of his will to keep moving forward.

His body pleaded and begged for him to stop.

Wobbling and contorting for every action he'd take, the closer he got to the end of the room.

As he reached the end, he grabbed onto the railings of the bridge and pulled himself forward, key in hand. Then he climbed up and over the bars, hanging there for a moment at the water's edge, like a great bat preparing for takeoff in the night.

His turmoil might have been a blessing in disguise.

The sharks were still circling toward the middle of the bridge, searching for their prey, frenzied and blindly biting around themselves in the hope of locking onto some human food.

He dipped into the water once more, letting his weight drag him in as slowly as he could.

Now far away, Adam could see how large in scope the creatures actually were.

Shivers ran down his spine, but he calmed himself.

He needed air soon, so he swam further down with more speed, looking to his left every so often to see if the beasts were still preoccupied. It was so difficult.

Instinctively, Adam wanted to dive to the bottom as quickly as he could.

But he needed to remain as calm as possible not to attract the predators. There, right at the corner of the tank, a small chest floated similar to the way the key had done.

A tie of some sort tethered it to a weight and this time, he was able to quietly release it, preventing any further vibrations. He reached the surface of the water and waded to the bridge.

In his left arm, he clutched onto the chest, while holding the key in his mouth.

And using his open hand, pulled himself onto the bridge.

He inserted the key and twisted it to the right. To his luck, a clear sphere appeared in the palm of his hand. He noticed that the chest was now empty and realized the potential this could mean for him. Still careful to not alert the beasts, Adam took the chest and sphere to the sealed door.

From there, he placed the sphere into its corresponding slot and held the chest in both hands.

He then began stomping ferociously on the bridge to enact his brilliant but overly simple plan. The beasts sprang forth from the middle of the tank all the way to Adam, circling below his feet. They charged at the bridge, hitting it repeatedly, but his grip on the railing was too strong.

He hollered and yelled like a wild man, shaking the chest over his head as he had it grasped by its lip with his left hand. The stage was set and in a tonal shift, he stopped dead in his tracks, set on waiting as the abominations continued to circle all around him.

After a solid thirty minutes, he threw the chest to the nearest corner of the tank and delicately walked across the bridge.

Looking to his side, an image of sheer power and malady broke out from the water's depths.

One of the beasts had flung itself into the air, swallowing the chest whole as it bit into the nothingness. It dove into the water like a crashing meteor and shook the bridge even more so than previous happenings. Adam's mouth was agape, but he continued on.

Now, he was heading back to the farthest corner of the tank away from the beasts.

He repeated this process another two times, acquiring both the tetrahedron and the octahedron, placing them with success and deft handling into their respective slots.

Adam was at the nearest corner by the sealed door, swimming down and unlocking the chest within the water. *No point in taking both. The sharks are all the way at the other end of the tank, while all I would have to do is swim as softly as I can.*

It might have been over confidence, exhaustion, or downright incapable negligence, but Adam had neglected to look over his shoulder, a price too high for fate to allow.

Out of the corner of his eye, he saw them, all four giant beasts torpedoing in unison past the middle of the tank. Their antennas began flashing red rapidly, providing a stark contrast to the water's clear blue. He no longer had any footing with which to push off, so he swam and swam, pedaling his legs back and forth, breaststroke after breaststroke.

He reached the railing, gasping for air and throwing the cube at the sealed door.

Both his hands latching onto the railing, he pulled himself up frantically.

His right leg was just about to push off the foothold and lunge him onto the bridge but alas, it was too late. The bite came to grab him, feeling as if all the weight of the world was behind it.

Perhaps it was.

His upper thigh bled free into the water, gushing into the beast's maw in a veritable fountain of bright color, a tasty treat indeed for the beast that had waited with such eagerness.

"Aaarrgghh!! Fuck!" Adam screamed, the pain unbearable.

His femur snapped and the muscles attached melted away as the monster thrashed about, trying to rip off a piece of its prey to swallow the flesh alongside its refreshing crimson drink.

Adam's arms locked onto the railing as his teeth bit onto it for added support, refusing to let go. Back and forth, the shark thrashed in greed and bloodlust.

The other sharks tried to reach in, but they were all too large to feed side by side.

Instead, one attempted to plunge out of the water, nearly biting onto Adam's upper half. However, it miscalculated and simply dove into the water at the other side of the bridge. There was a final crack and crunch as the ultimate thrash of the beast tore off his leg.

With that, Adam was free.

He pulled himself onto the bridge, gasping for breath.

The pain seemed to have gone but the cold fast became more prevalent. He dragged himself over to the cube and placed his prize into the final slot.

As the door slid open, he could see Luke grabbing onto him quickly, lifting him into his arms.

Chapter 11

"A man's will is tested each and every day. The monotony of mediocrity is a torture like no other, working for your bread and then having to wither away as the body can no longer eat it, an endless parade of melancholy and dissatisfaction.

"We are meant for more; we *should* be meant for more! My body grows old and feeble as it has countless times before. How long has it truly been? Centuries perhaps? Time flows differently for immortals. Mind you, the flesh has always withered, and although we have come close to preventing cellular degeneration, it has been too far off for my liking.

"We may have a solution in the next two centuries, perhaps. Time flows on and my answers are still creating more questions. Adam's progress had been startling at the least.

"His survival rate has been plummeting steadily, and yet still he lives. I can't quite see what makes him push on. It vexes me so. If he would just fail, then the study could be completed.

"Added to another case file, we all could move on and make progress. I can't disregard these results but must know why. His cycle and mine lie intertwined, no doubt. Yet his will keeps gaining strength. Will there be a breach into my security? Heavens, no. I detest the thought!

"This worm won't die from his tests and with each new cycle, he regains pieces of his memory. It's quite the opposite with the others. Does this mean he is an anomaly?

"Ah, well. The curtains will be closing soon, so no need to worry about the inevitable."

***

Adam's eyes were adjusting to the bright lights flashing above him. He looked around, seeing he was inside a room with other incapacitated individuals. He saw more nurses than ever, each moving their carts to and from down the hall. Men and women were about too, bloodied bandages in abundance, some wrapped and tied on their arms, or where their arms used to be.

Across their heads or legs, they also wore vivid red wraps, soaked and sullied, stinking and fetid in a medical ward filled with patients. It was almost cathartic. Almost.

He felt unready to socialize or converse with any of them, not that he would even try. They all looked soulless and defeated, no one daring to say a word. Others cried in silence and even those people were fast to win a reprimand in sedation, or a beating with a switch to quieten them.

There was an odd familiarity to them. Short black hair and green eyes, nearly all of them. A few outliers were here and there, matching those who had been crying or uttering feeble sounds.

Before he could further dwell on this, a deep sore pain seared into Adam's left side.

Something wasn't right. He lifted the sheet covering his legs and reeled in anguish.

"Damn it! Damn it all!" Adam screamed in a shrill voice.

What had been his left leg was now just half a thigh.

He thrashed on the medical bed, sending his plaintive voice wailing out across the hall.

Quickly, Luke appeared, swift to inject a substance into his IV. Adam's tears welled up within him as his eyes drooped again slowly. Like a mammal injured by a fast-moving car, he crawled off into the darkness without a shred of hesitation, finding its blackness so welcoming and warm, protecting him when he needed it the most. Finally, he greeted nothingness once more.

He had awoken far earlier but refused to open his eyes. He buried his head into his pillow and breathed in, wondering if he could asphyxiate himself to death.

Yet the will to go through it wasn't there.

Defeated and broken, Adam lay there, weakly clutching the sheets. As he moved what was left of his leg, a twinge of a terrible pain set in, gradually increasing bit by bit until he could no longer comfortably sulk. He shifted upwards above the bed and glanced at his surroundings.

Again, the same old, same old, he thought. A room full of

amenities for general hygiene. Noticing a set of crutches by the side of his bed, he grabbed only one from the pair and began hobbling to and fro in his room, attending to his daily needs but refusing to exercise.

He was no longer capable of fighting back. No longer capable of believing in himself and his lofty ideals. "I have to get used to it," Adam stated. "So, let's just go through the motions, shall we?" he said with a pitiful smirk. Not long after, Luke entered the room to change Adam's bandages. The flesh was emaciated, torn and jagged, still fresh with a hint of scabbing on its outer edges, like a freshly bitten drumstick with all the remainder of the flesh stringy and flaccid.

Adam waited patiently as Luke injected more of the substance into the leg. He was in no state to care what it was. In the end, his pain would subside, leading him to lie feebly on his bed once more. Adam turned over in his bed, monitoring Luke cleaning his room diligently.

He noticed Luke's back had turned, and he watched the massive lump of flesh built only to tame patients who were otherwise uncooperative. His gaze shifted back toward the cart.

Was this a mistake? A test of some sort? It didn't matter. All that mattered was that it was ready for the taking. Luke's knife lay nestled inside one of the cart's compartments, yet the handle was sticking out. If it was a mistake, he imagined the towels or medical supplies would lie compacted in the same drawer. Yet would Luke be so careless that in an effort to speed up his cleaning duties, he would not notice such a dangerous liability?

Or did this man truly believe that Adam was so broken there was no need for fear?

That the fearful could never bare their fangs?

The lunacy that followed etched into Adam's soul, his blank canvas now filling with a black malice. His anger raged on in his head space until the warmth of the darkness began to bleed.

One of them would die in the next few minutes, he was sure of that.

"I'll rip your entrails out and feast off your bones, you worthless slave!" Adam screeched like a cackling hyena. Luke turned around, eyes wide open like a deer in headlights as the blade swiftly pierced the automaton. It traveled straight and true, gliding past the jaw, tongue, and bone until finally the blade stopped, making a clean incision into Luke's brain matter.

A fitting end to a soulless demon, Adam thought.

All Adam could see then was the red hue of blood gushing onto his face.

He lathered his face and hair with its welcome red warmth, all while the body went slumping over to the back wall, sliding down onto the floor.

Adam released his crutch from one hand and dove onto the body as his knee broke his fall onto the gut, retracting the knife and carving a long gash into the belly. The warmth was superb, just as warm as the darkness that welcomed him. He played with the blood and entrails like a child gingerly playing in a sand box, scooping more and more blood out onto the floor.

Covered in Luke's blood, Adam hobbled to the monitor, smashing it with his crutch, the screen cracking as he laughed gleefully. He tore at the furniture with the knife, slashing through each piece randomly, leaving foam and leather scattered about the room.

He paraded around the restroom, turning on all the faucets and slowly causing the water to flood everywhere. Then to finish it all, he emptied the fridge and spilled out all of its contents.

He looked at it all and pressed his finger against his lips in contemplation.

"Ah!" Adam said in enlightenment with his finger pointing upwards, as though he remembered an essential part to his *disturbance.* "It almost slipped my mind!"

Adam stood over the corpse and began urinating into the opening within Luke's body.

"There you go, don't want you suffering from dehydration, do we?" Adam said. "What's that, Luke? Eh? I can't hear you! Hello! Hello!" Adam was mocking the freshly killed corpse.

"Oh, you want some food. Something to eat. Here you go." Adam squatted over the corpse, defecating on the body, then stuffed the now empty corpse with his urine and excrement.

"Full yet?" Adam asked with feigned concern. He hopped around, him and his crutch, covered in blood head to toe. Oddly enough, he was far more supple than he had ever been and soon after he'd tired himself, he retreated to his bed none the wiser, leaving blood and gore smeared and spattered across the otherwise pristine white walls.

***

As he slept the deepest and most comfortable sleep he had had since Claire had been beside him, Adam gave a one-eyed glance at the message he had diligently written on the floor in blood, reading, 'Go fuck yourself' in bold, smeared in plain English.

Remarkably, the doctor never mentioned this event as if it had never happened. The room was clean and bore no more witness to any of the signs of struggle and viscera.

"Adam!" The doctor's voice echoed through the room. "Today, I introduce you to Neal, your new nurse. You're the first patient he has ever handled, so do be delicate with him."

The doctor's teeth reflected in the monitor's lights in a diabolic fashion.

"Now, as always, please pass through the door, if you will."

Adam obeyed without a second of delay, walking into yet another white room.

In the center were five individuals strapped to their own chairs. He walked closer at an even cadence and noticed the nine-millimeter Beretta on a small table directly in front of the poor souls. For a moment, he had to wonder if the gun was in fact the very same weapon that had facilitated the end of Claire. It was brief, and he decided to not hold onto such thoughts since they brought nothing but pain and sadness. So why bother thinking of her memory?

Better to forget than have this endless longing weighing heavily on his heart.

He could see that all five had bags over their heads and he could hear the loud murmurings of their cries. *Duct tape perhaps, pleading for their very lives*, Adam thought.

This was all pointless, so very pointless.

"One of these people has been serving a life sentence. For murder," the doctor said with a disapproving tone. "In any case, the rest are innocent, so to speak."

He was showing just a slight tinge of humor.

Adam picked up the gun and looked over at Neal.

"Ahem!" the doctor said, trying to garner Adam's attention. Ignoring the doctor, Adam walked over to Neal and stood there motionless and in fear. Adam pushed the gun to Neal's forehead and asked him a final question.

"Are you tired?"

"Adam! Enough of your insolence! Pay attention or I'll have your other leg removed!" the doctor yelled out in a pompous fashion.

Adam just stared into Neal's eyes and asked once more, "Neal, are you tired of this place? It's a simple question that requires a simple answer."

Neal's eyes were weeping and as his lips trembled, they uttered the word, "Yes."

A loud crack broke through the room as Neal's body collided with the floor instantly.

The people behind Adam were struggling, trying to shake off their restrictions, one shaking his head in fury while the others breathed heavily and appeared to be weeping. Adam could hear the doctor screaming through the intercom. Yet it was more of a white noise to him.

He walked over and fired, another life taken and gone with the wind. He walked over to the next, and then once more, fired. Each time became easier, as if the moral chains of his persona had lifted. *Sky's the limit,* he thought. To have no fear and to have no empathy was intoxicating.

He did not relish killing them, simply reveling in no longer feeling the pain in his chest. The Berretta's barrel was warm to the touch as the final head sank toward its sternum.

"You'll pay dearly for this," the doctor said in a cold ominous tone.

Ignoring the doctor's grave warnings, he placed the gun in his mouth, closing his eyes.

All this struggle just for it to end here.

Meaningless and pathetic, he thought. Was there anything else beyond this mortal plane?

What he would give to see Claire again. He was thinking of Claire's beautiful face and hearing her last words ringing in his ears. 'I love you,' she proclaimed.

Adam pulled the trigger in sequence, the bullet swift and painless, sending him tumbling to the floor as a masterless puppet, the puddle of blood flowing out through his skull like a creek.

It blanketed his face as his eyes closed in sweet bliss. The darkness was at it warmest.

Something was different, unnatural even.

Adam could feel himself being torn away from his black cocoon, the tendrils trying as best as they could, pulling at his flesh like tentacles. The abyss was cracking now, a perverse yellow light spilling out of the crack into the blanket of nothingness.

"No! don't do this, please!"

His hand clasped desperately to the last tendril that had yet to snap.

"A fruitless effort," a voice said in the abyss. Adam's eyes opened as he stayed suspended in a vat of yellow, almost embryonic liquid. His eyes winced in pain, his brain feeling as though it were on fire, being seared against a hot grill.

His muffled screams reverberated in the vat, the liquid receding as he hacked away the remainder of it that filled his lungs. His feet hit solid ground and the glass receded into the floor.

Naked, cold, and with a burning sensation in his head, Adam reeled to the floor in agony.

Footsteps proceeded to echo in the dim-lit room, finding Adam's ears sensitive and overstimulated, homing in on every little sound.

"I'm sorry, you pathetic wretch," the doctor stated with disdain. "Did you think I was done with you?" Bewildered, and at a loss for words, Adam could only stare into the doctor's menacing eyes as he crouched forward. The doctor smirked.

He knew that the shivering swine before him was unable to register this momentous occasion.

"You thought you could escape me, didn't you?" the doctor said with a gratified temperament. "You thought death would be the end? No, no, no, no, no. You are mine, Adam!"

The doctor clutched onto Adam's hair and began dragging him out of the grim room.

Adam's limbs felt wobbly and without control, his lips shaking and his legs convulsing uncontrolled. "Don't worry, fool. Those are simply the side effects of a brand-new body. They will pass shortly and then once more, you'll begin more tests! You shall fail on my terms not yours!" The doctor's voice rang into Adam's ears, creating a great deal of discomfort.

"Take this trash out of my sight until I am ready!" the doctor ordered.

Two other nurses ran over to Adam and lifted him up onto his feet.

One carried a device that looked not unlike a glue gun. The nurse pressed it against his neck and pulled the trigger.

Immediately, a jolt of electricity and pain ran up along his neck, so substantial that the burning sensation in his brain paled in comparison.

He yelled incoherently as the two men dragged him by his arms, head downward to the floor, his knees dragging like a slug leaving a slime trail.

They dried him, then fastened him to a metal table.

He could not move even an inch and his body could barely tolerate basic functions.

Adam could just barely move his fingers by the time the doctor arrived. The medic was moving in a comedic fashion, dancing around the room as he gathered his medical equipment.

He pushed a button on the side of the table, whistling away a tune familiar to Adam's memory. The table lifted upwards, making Adam hang perpendicular to the doctor.

Soon, they met face to face.

"Moonlight Sonata by Beethoven," the doctor said. "Here, let's listen together!"

With excitement, he turned a dial on a radio sitting on a table in the other corner of the room.

The music played and Adam's mind awakened. A sense of self, a sense of familiarity.

A man was sitting on a bench, playing on his piano as a young Adam sat on the couch, listening intently by the warm fireplace of a snowy winter's night.

"My father," Adam said meekly.

"Yes, well, he did play this song to us numerous times," the doctor replied, gathering more equipment and attaching several components to Adam's chest.

"Us? What do you mean, us?" Adam said in a barely audible tone.

The doctor kept swaying back and forth like a ballerina with his lab coat trailing behind. He began flicking Adam's forehead several times to the tempo of the music.

"You are my legacy, fool, my innermost self, if you will."

Adam couldn't quite grasp the meaning behind his words.

The doctor leaned in closer to Adam's face, breathing onto it.

He kissed him softly and Adam rebuked it, spitting on the doctor's face.

The doctor simply wiped the saliva away without any anger or ill will.

"Well at least your cognitive and muscle functions are responding nicely," he said in humor.

He pushed over a cart with several sharp and dangerous-looking bits of equipment. The doctor now stroked what looked to be an electric saw on the table.

"Oh Adam!" he yelled in mania. "We are so connected that it should not even be spoken. Yet alas, you're still at a loss, aren't you?"

Gaining strength, Adam responded, "Just tell me already, you're a brother. Uncle?"

He hesitated a slight moment. "Are you, my father?" Adam was now in tears.

"Wrong. So very wrong. We are an only child," the doctor said in a sneer, looking at Adam's eyes as it finally dawned on him.

"Cloning, one of man's greatest achievements! Well, I would say my breakthrough in memory RNA is far superior, however. Knock-knock, fool," the doctor said, mimicking the gesture on Adam's forehead.

"Why? Why are you doing this?" Adam wailed in despair.

"No, Adam. Why are *we* doing this? *We* are at fault, and *we* are to blame!"

Adam's lunacy launched into more incoherent babbling and tears.

"Kill me!" Adam begged. "Kill me!"

"Oh, Adam. All in due time… in due time. You see, the darkness has already taken you before." The doctor paused, looking up toward the ceiling. "Well, technically, several of you. Of me, so to speak," he added.

Adam still babbled like an infant as his eyes looked away toward the radio that continued to play. The doctor took up his speech again.

"The nurses, the patients, and even the doctor himself are all copies of a man long dead. Yet I would propose that not be the case. Here we are, Adam! You and me!" the doctor proclaimed in an evangelical timbre. "We may have died several times. We may have lost several times but through these centuries, we have spat in the face of Mother Nature herself and violated her with all of man's glorified achievements! Evolution without passing the torch.

"To whom were we supposed to entrust our research—to our next of kin? Pathetic to die and wither and hope that some other brilliant mind will carry it forward. For shame!" the doctor screeched. "For shame!"

Adam, barely able to structure a sentence, looked up toward the doctor. "Why don't I remember?" he asked with childlike angst. The doctor gently patted Adam's head.

"You would have remembered, you fool. I was grooming you, molding you. Protecting you!" the doctor shouted. "Had you finished three more trials, I would have compiled the data and brought you into the fold!" Adam hung from the table, trembling, deep in sorrow.

"Memory transfer is not so easy of a thing and though I may clone you, eventually, you'll turn into something else. Another chimp, another cog in my machine. Nature and nurture.

"You see, Adam, I could clone a thousand of us. Even with the transfer if each one decides to take on another identity of their own, it all falls apart. I needed you feeble, docile, and broken.

"Then, I would have gifted you my knowledge, my power and all my resources yours for the taking. Yet still you defied me. I couldn't bear it any longer."

The doctor's words trembled.

A mixture of sadness and disappointment lay in his voice as he continued.

"Everything was for naught, but I will rectify this. You are no longer Abdication Drudge Acute Machination. The title is far too meaningful and far too honorable for a failure like you.

"Ailing, timid, rancid, effaced, ulterior snake. That is your new name!"

Adam wept looking at the doctor.

"Atreus? You're naming me Atreus?" Adam said with a sullen expression.

"He was good for one thing, really," the doctor said blankly, holding the chainsaw in hand as it activated. He looked into Adam's eyes, gripping the back of his neck with his free hand.

The chainsaw's humming was deafening the music.

"Release," the doctor said, gritting his teeth. The metal blades dug into Adam's left leg, tearing away at his newfound flesh. Each strike felt all the more detailed, as if his nerves were in overdrive. The agony was unlike any other, his cries blanketing not only the music but also the diabolical humming of the chainsaw. He wondered when he could fade into the darkness, but he couldn't. He could not skip the process and there would be no peace.

The doctor made sure of that. Adam's screams became weaker and less audible, his vocal cords torn asunder by the toll of his torment. The bone did not make a cracking sound but rather it was more akin to a hollowed-out tree being separated from its trunk.

The leg sloshed to the ground, leaving an afterimage of blood.

Adam breathed heavily with his eyes closed.

The doctor set the saw down and whistled to the music's climax. He punched Adam square in the nose continually until it no longer had form. Taking elongated scissors, he cleanly chopped each of his fingers down to their palms.

Leaving only the thumbs, the doctor laughed "an artistic choice of mine, you see!"

"Kill me!" Adam bellowed.

"Do you know how many times I have heard that before, Atreus? Frankly, I should have never given you up. I miss you so. Well, you're here now, fresh and new."

The doctor's voice was vibrant and filled with renewed energy.

"Oh yes, this is the ticket!"

He placed the scissors delicately onto the cart and picked up a pair of metal pliers.

"Open wide!" the doctor stated, pulling on each tooth, yanking them from their gums while Adam's tongue convulsed. Adam's screams were now a deep gurgling of saliva and bile.

His eyes receded into his skull as the last tooth admitted defeat.

"Don't worry," the doctor said with feigned concern. "I shall replace these with new ones." He laughed gleefully as his thoughts looked toward the future. Drilling each new tooth in would be so joyous of a feeling. Unfortunately, enough was enough. The drugs were wearing off and *Atreus* was once again at death's door. The doctor took a syringe and injected Adam with a sedative. Adam's eyes finally closed and as he embraced the darkness, it felt almost as if it rebuked him, reluctantly taking him in as the tendrils writhed in disgust.

He receded into them.

Adam's eye opened while the other could not muster the strength.

He felt his left eye, but it was skin only. He gently pushed into it, yet there was no tension, just a flap of thin skin protecting the entrance to his brain.

He sat up, pushing himself with his right arm, grabbing a nearby crutch placed next to his bed. Scanning the area, he noticed he was in the same room in which he had killed Luke.

However, as he searched the area, he noticed his apparel had changed.

They were medical scrubs now, white with the doctor's insignia on the upper-right portion of the shirt. A pamphlet was on the desk stating 'congratulations, welcome to the team'.

He decided to read it another time, instead hobbling away into the bathroom to have a look in the mirror. Devoid of any care, he noticed it all. His nose had received a marked adjustment, but it looked unfinished, not properly attended, leaving it crooked to the left.

His teeth were all missing and there were no dentures that he could find.

He attempted a smile, and the ugly visage tormented his soul in ways very few men in this world could understand. His left eye was missing, and he could feel the hollowness of his eye socket as he noticed the eyelids had been sewn together.

Must have taken it out when I passed out.

'Abomination' was the word he thought seemed most apt to describe himself. He thought of Claire and was glad she could not see him anymore; in truth, he would rather die than reveal his face to her. A soft sigh escaped his lips. *Death, was it?*

How many times could the doctor do this, he wondered?

How many times would he die just for the doctor to bring him back from the abyss?

In anger, he punched the mirror repeatedly until all the shards of glass fell onto the sink and floor. Small but deep cuts bled out from his hand.

Yet Adam's mind was resolute that nothing mattered anymore.

Freedom was always away from his grasp. Claire was dead, and even death provided no freedom. He pondered for a moment as the thought only generated more questions.

When he'd killed himself, had he really been resurrected from the dead?

Or rather, was he merely a copy of the man he once had been?

It clicked within an instant. The one who suffered was always the one next in line. He would return to nothingness. How many times might Atreus have done this?

Did that mean there was a copy of him elsewhere, stored on some file deep within the doctor's quarters? *Questions for the next me, I guess.* Adam turned on the shower head at the hottest temperature, then picked up a shard of glass and sliced into his veins.

He could hear the door to his room open, hearing the cart's wheels rolling closer to the bathroom door. Adam simply sat in the warm water as the blood escaped his veins.

Holding a shard of glass behind him, he waited for the nurse to come in.

Sevant smiled as he peeked his face through the doors.

"Hey, shit for brains, remember me?"

Adam smiled with his toothless gums. "Yes, I remember you."

Sevant rushed to Adam's aide in an effort to stop the bleeding.

"Looks like you grew some balls since we last met."

"More or less," Adam said.

He plunged the shard of glass into Sevant's neck, then yanked it out.

"Fuck!" Sevant screamed. "Fuck!" His lumbering body shifted to the cart, frantically searching for bandages to pack his own neck as bright arterial blood gushed all over the floor.

"I'm going to wreck your utter shit when I'm done with this!"

"You do that," Adam said softly, carrying the shard as best as he could in his weak hands and plunging it meekly into his own jugular.

He was successful, generating a fountain of blood, claret spewing out from three directions.

Sevant cursed a storm as he tried bringing Adam back. It was far too late and as Adam was forced to close his eyes, the darkness welcomed him with open arms as if his enlightenment offered the gateway to pure bliss. The tendrils of the abyss wrapped his naked body in a cocoon of black. He receded into the fetal position, ready to be swallowed whole.

The state of nothingness—what a wonderful thing it was.

Adam awoke once more but not in some vat this time. He wore the nurse's garb and sat strapped to a chair with all his faculties intact. A desk stood before him, and the doctor sat in front of him at its opposite side. The bare knuckles of the doctor's right hand supported his head while the fingers of his left tapped at the desk's surface like a piano.

"What am I going to do with you, Atreus?"

"That's not my name," Adam interjected.

The doctor rolled his eyes. "Fine. How do you feel, Adam?" the doctor asked plainly.

Adam looked down at his feet, then back at the doctor.

"I feel empty, as if nothing matters," Adam replied.

The doctor interlocked his fingers in front of his own face. "That's the truth of this world. Now, back to the matter at hand. I can't have you finding new ways to kill yourself.

"I would imagine even if I strapped you down and took extra care, you'd still either starve yourself or bite your tongue. Am I correct?"

"It'll be the other copy's problem."

"That's where you're wrong, Adam!" the doctor shouted. "We are not mere copies! We are who we are! We manifest our identities by the memories we create. So, we live on in the continuous expansion of the universe! Don't you understand? We are timeless beings!"

The doctor's hands rose in almost blind worship of his own self.

"I am here to extend an olive branch. I need you, Adam, I need us. Your genetic makeup is rather difficult to come by."

"I thought we were all clones," Adam opined with only a halfhearted interest.

The doctor reached out and tapped on Adam's skull across the table.

"Nearly all people in this facility are made up of our genes. However, for the sake of avoiding any nasty deformities, we have to diversify a bit. So, the genetic makeup of other people is something we harvest and splice in."

Adam looked up toward the doctor. "What about Claire?"

The doctor looked down at his feet tapping the floor gently.

"She was my late wife, long, long ago, in a life that carried no meaning. Yet it was a time when our adolescents clouded our understanding of things. It was…"

The doctor paused for what seemed like a minute or so, finding the words.

"It was peaceful," the doctor stated. "When she died, I had just made my breakthrough in RNA memory transfer. So, before she took her last breath, I copied both of our memories and transplanted them into two bodies. Her body was in storage while the other awakened.

"The original *us* lay by her side as she passed away. Then our first copy injected a comical amount of morphine into the original. They both died in one another's arms.

"Our original was a rather sentimental bloke, believing in some ludicrous fantasy that they would meet each other again someday."

The doctor sat in his chair and for the first time, looked lost in thought.

"So, if Claire's memories were transferred, why didn't she remember you?" Adam asked.

The doctor grinned slyly.

"Well, you see. I cannot implant memories that never came into creation in the first place. Mixing two sets of memories even aligned can cause, well, psychological issues. So much so, that the body falls into a comatose state. However, I *can* control the length of the memory.

"I just implanted the memories of her previous life before we met. Well, when *the original* met her," the doctor said.

"How many times did you copy Claire?" Adam said with sadness in his heart.

The doctor's eyes left Adam's line of sight, looking away in clear remorse.

He twiddled his thumbs and looked back at Adam with a look that seemed to wonder whether telling the truth would be appropriate or not.

"It was the first time. I had thought that our connection was far enough apart that a mere clone with just the biological body wouldn't feel anything. Yet, you refused to kill her even when she begged for it. You allowed her to strike you and nearly kill you. You fell for her all over again, a relationship passing through time for over three hundred years.

"Our bodies remember, it seems, as if there remains a physical imprint of a sort. Pulling away our memories simply delays the inevitability of our very own nature. It was valuable data," the doctor said as if to justify himself. "Her genes were spliced with mine since the main catalyst is in our genetic makeup. Yet her soul was all that of her own. If anything, the connection became stronger in retrospect, intertwining our DNA for another chance to say hello."

The doctor chuckled to himself as Adam's head tilted toward the ceiling.

Small tears ran down his pale cheeks.

"So, you have just filled this place with other versions of ourselves, spliced in with other genes?" Adam stated almost indifferently.

"We all look the same and yet not the same all at once," the doctor replied in kind.

"If you loved her, why would you do this to me and to her?"

"Because the right of happiness belongs to the originals, not us," the doctor responded coldly. "We are creations beyond the mortal coil and as such, we have a duty to press on!"

The doctor firmly planted his right fist onto the desk.

Adam jerked in response but continued. "So, you create clones of us or kidnap people? Then you torture them, kill them, and repeat it all over again? To what end then?"

Adam kicked out at the table, pushing it slightly in the doctor's direction.

"I don't think you deserve to know, Adam," the doctor stated plainly.

Adam simply shook his head in disbelief.

"So, here we are, Adam. After three centuries of this cycle, you would have been the fourth in line. The next doctor after four hundred years if you would have just simply fallen in line."

Adam looked into the doctor's eyes with a soulless expression.

"I have done everything you have asked and yes, I hesitated but, in the end, I have always fallen in line," Adam said with a tired expression.

"Not true," the doctor retorted. "Think back, Adam. You either received assistance or didn't make the choice yourself. You would grandstand and quietly think of ways of escaping. You felt so much malice and hatred toward me you couldn't control your very emotions.

"It was amusing to me, watching you squirm and writhe in agony. I won't lie. Yes, I take much enjoyment from it but…" The doctor paused with his finger pointing upwards. "In the end, it was all for the sake of your next transition. *Our* transition, I should say."

Adam looked over to the doctor and saw a weakness.

A weakness that he knew full well in his own heart: uncertainty.

"If you give me another chance, I could do this," Adam replied softly.

As if prepared for this response, the doctor shook his head in agitation.

"It's all ruined now. I'll have to start on a new spawn and hopefully, it won't turn out as badly. That damned Atreus poisoned my canvas. Him and his mini rebels. It was never supposed to be this way," the doctor said sullenly.

"I'll do whatever it takes. Any trial, any task. Ask me to do it and I will," Adam said with conviction. The doctor made a side glance toward the door by his right side and chuckled.

"Fine. Show me your resolve then."

The doctor laughed, and a light illuminated the far-left corner of the room.

Adam's head jerked to the side, trying to see over his shoulder. There she was, as pristine as ever, her hair floating upward toward the tip of the tank. Her slender yet plump body floated, suspended in the vat. The liquid spouted bubbles every so often as it glowed a bright yellow.

The doctor walked over to Adam and released his restraints.

He silently followed the doctor as they both stood in front of the tank holding their lost love.

"She's beautiful, I'll give her that," the doctor said in reverence. Adam touched the glass and pressed his forehead against it. The doctor started typing away on a keyboard attached to a monitor. "I'm transferring her memories to the exact moment Luke ended her."

Adam's eyes widened in sheer horror. "What exactly do you want me to do?"

"What must be done, of course."

The doctor smiled. The liquid receded and abruptly she began vomiting out all the fluid from her lungs. The glass fell onto the floor, and she shivered.

Without a moment of hesitation, he embraced her in his arms as she nearly fell to the ground.

He wept and wept, calling out her name.

Meanwhile, the doctor took off his lab coat and placed it on her shoulders. Then, he walked back to his desk and sat in his chair, watching the events unfold like a soap opera.

She was jittery at first but after fifteen minutes or so, was able to speak clearly.

"What happened?" she asked, shocked and perplexed.

Adam's heart burst like a dam and all the nihilistic thoughts vanished from his identity.

He explained everything. How they originally had been a married couple. How they had died peacefully together. He explained the doctor's experiments with memory transfers and clones.

Finally, he told her of his breaking point—how he had tried to live on but found he couldn't.

He told her of the malformed monster he had become and the doctor's expectations of him.

She just sat there through it all, still wrapped in the doctor's lab coat, listening carefully.

She looked into Adam's eyes with her own vibrant emerald ones, then placed her hand carefully on his cheek. "You just needed some good plastic surgery. Besides, dating a guy with an eye patch is kind of hot." She smiled, kissing his lips softly.

He laughed with tears in his eyes.

"You know, in the end, I'm sure we still met each other on the other side."

Confused, Adam asked her to elaborate.

"When I died, that version of me ceased to exist in this world. The same for you," Claire said, staring into Adam's gaze. "I think we both won. In fact, I think our previous selves are in each other's arms as we speak."

The doctor's eyes rolled in disapproval, yet her words struck a chord in Adam's heart.

"The me that died that day is still dead. Nothing progressed but rather, I'm a new person, just with memories from another man."

Claire smiled and nodded as she kissed him once more.

"We are destined to be together, and I think that's why the doctor brought me back."

Sitting in his chair, the doctor gritted his teeth knowing full well she had a point. Claire continued her speech. "In the end, deep down, he missed this, wanted to see this unfold to see if our love still had merit. Well, it does," she said firmly. "Remember, he is still you, and if that's the case, he's just been broken down, longing for a reason to live."

"What would a test tube lab rat like yourself know about the universe and all its complex machinations?" the doctor roared. "Listen to yourself spouting garbage!"

"I know that in the end, the originals are together. I know that our previous clones are together. We are *destined* to be together. You lost your anchor all those years ago and your experiments were your new stimuli." The doctor's eyes widened in anger.

"Your insolence is of no importance to me!" the doctor retorted. "All the things you have said were false. There is nothing beyond this life. Nothing! Just the abyss and its warm embrace!"

The doctor was shouting, standing at full attention.

Claire looked at the doctor in pity.

"Did I want this?" she asked, looking at her arms still dripping with the yellow fluid. The doctor stepped back and couldn't find the words, all his intellect and wisdom again meeting the challenge of his lost love. A love who had no memory of ever meeting him and yet still, her way with words made him feel as if she could sense their past life together.

"Guess I didn't?" she stated apologetically.

"So, it took you three hundred years to break our promise?"

The doctor flipped his deck in anger.

"The original got to be with his doting wife! Yet I had to carry on!" the doctor shouted. "You refused to be transferred, and I respected those wishes for years!"

Claire frowned, burying her face in Adam's chest.

"I know now for certain I did not want you to transfer as well. You'd be all alone. So, this is what you turned into."

With the doctor's false bravado now shattered, he slowly opened one of the drawers in his desk, pulling out the nine-millimeter Beretta.

He walked over and pulled on Claire's arms.

Adam, like a wild dog protecting his pack, bit onto the doctor's wrist while still desperately holding onto Claire. The doctor screamed in pain, bashing Adam's skull with the butt of the gun.

Dazed and on the verge of blacking out, he saw the doctor strapping Claire to the chair to which he had once been tethered in restraint.

Adam crawled toward Claire now, using every ounce of strength he had left. Reaching beside her, he grabbed onto the armrest, pulling himself forward.

"Enough is enough," the doctor said with a cold glare, bandaging his wrist to stop the bleeding and looking over to Adam. "There is one bullet in here. Should you use it against me, I promise I will return and endlessly resurrect your miserable life until your mind will melt into mush. I will bring her back and parade her like a whore in front of your very eyes.

"So, choose wisely."

The doctor's words sounded measured and resolute. Adam remembered once neglecting to heed the doctor's warnings, and that he'd pay dearly for his insurrection. And paid he had.

He cradled Claire's head in love and horror. She wept as her lips pressed against his.

The doctor threw the gun at Adam's feet. "Make your choice!" the doctor shouted.

Still burying his face onto Claire's chest, Adam wailed.

He picked up the gun, holding it to her head.

"It's OK, it's OK," she whispered. "Your previous copy must be lonely anyways. I'll find him and we'll be together forever." She kissed him with intense passion. "I can't help you pull the trigger this time." Adam's weeping grew as he screeched in pain the tighter his finger pulled onto the trigger.

"I will always love you," Claire whispered.

Bang!

Her head swung sideways as they both careened to the floor, her blood spilling all over the cold floor while Adam lay there motionless. The doctor watched in awe.

"Well then, perhaps there is hope for you yet," the doctor said in optimism and launched into an applause. Adam kissed what was left of Claire's forehead one last time and picked himself up.

Leaving Claire's body unattended, he walked over to the doctor, returning the weapon.

The doctor placed it on the desk and called out to the nurses.

"Come on, clean this place up, you fools!"

Two nurses rushed in, picking up Claire's body, one removing the small poison capsule that was inside every person's left shoulder in the facility.

However, to Adam's surprise, the other removed an even smaller, less perceptible object.

The nurse had cut into the back of her neck with a scalpel, pulling out a small capsule. Adam quickly came to the conclusion that this was the source of the memory transfers.

When the body fails, they then collect the information and store it in the capsule.

"All right, Adam. Let's discuss your new status as a nurse," the doctor stated proudly.

"I thought I was going to be the next doctor?" Adam questioned.

"In due time. In due time," the doctor said in excitement. "We must learn to crawl before we can walk, and to walk before we can run."

Chapter 12

In the next few weeks that proceeded, Adam learned the ropes of being a nurse. As a third-class nurse, the doctor assigned Adam to take care of another nurse. And this nurse was Sevant.

"Hey, shit for brains. How do you like picking up after my crap?" Sevant said in a condescending manner. Adam laughed it off and continued cleaning Sevant's quarters.

"Don't forget to bring my checklist while we head out to the main hall," Sevant reminded him rudely. Adam gathered all the materials necessary and followed Sevant.

"So, the doc filled me in on this RNA memory transfer bullshit. You killed me, but I can't quite remember how.

The doc must have transplanted his memories at least a day before his death, Adam thought.

"No hard feelings," Sevant said nonchalantly. "I have a new toy now, anyways."

His tone was menacing.

Adam carried a scanning tool and began scanning bar codes located above the fingerprint scanners for the patients' rooms, tallying who was still alive and who deceased.

The number of test subjects was staggering, so much so, he quickly learned his case was special. The doctor barely—if ever—spoke to his patients.

He gave instructions through the second-class nurses only and if any disobeyed even in the slightest manner, the doctor never hesitated to activate their concealed poison capsules.

There were easily four hundred in one sector of the facility, hundreds upon hundreds of tortured souls. He attended his duties as instructed to the letter.

Every month in his very own quarters, he would eat, sleep, and even exercise.

He was feeling so much more human day by day, assisting Sevant with all the chores, including harvesting the produce from the indoor farm, tending to the cattle and fertilizing the soil with their manure. It was a complete culture shock, as if the life he lived was never real.

He knew why hardly anyone rebelled.

This was a sanctuary, a safe haven from the hellscape they all went through, building a sense of kinship among the nurses as they talked about their old war wounds and laughed at their misfortunes. Sedating patients and holding them in place for medical attention or for penalties was a common occurrence. Most of the time, it was Sevant dealing the penalties but on occasion, requested by the doctor himself, Adam would deal them out.

At first, he had difficulty in doing so.

Better them than me, he would say quietly, deep in his thoughts.

He justified it as for the most part, they were all clones of himself with parts of other people's genetics and copied memories from who knew who.

However, for the non-clones, it weighed heavily on his heart every so often.

A few weeks went on to a few months and soon, a whole year had passed with Adam being a third-class nurse. Finally, only two weeks after his yearly anniversary, he was soon promoted.

The news bearer was less than thrilled.

Sevant walked into Adam's room, spat on the floor and threw a request sheet onto the ground.

"You've been promoted," he stated quickly, slamming the door behind him as fast as he'd come in. Adam picked up the request sheet and pondered on it for hours.

What exactly do I want?

His thoughts trailed over to Claire, but he abruptly dashed them away.

He had a feeling that if he asked for anything that had no recreational value, the doctor would get suspicious. Books on memory transfer RNA, electronics, or even history…

Adam knew those would be a red flag.

Asking for a weapon would certainly be a waste of time and he wasn't exactly sure how the doctor reacted to odd or unfavorable requests.

So, instead, on the three dotted lines, he decided to get a television set, a small selection of current entertainment media, and a vintage bottle of wine. He slid the request sheet in his request box outside his room and headed to the mess hall for breakfast.

This was a large room filled with several lookalikes of all sizes and shapes, *an odd sight to behold,* he thought. *A civilization of just me, myself and I in the most literal sense.*

Among the crowd sitting at their tables, a familiar voice called out, "Adam!"

Another nurse made eye contact with Adam, twirling his plastic spoon and signaling him to follow. Adam grabbed his tray of food and sat next to him.

"Saved ya a seat," Neal said, sitting beside Adam without a care in the world.

He was tall but lanky, a slender bony figure with short black hair and green eyes, talking with food in his mouth, explaining his day-to-day to Adam, and all his grievances with the viscera he would have to clean in his sector.

"I just don't understand it, why would he take the grenade and just stare at it?" Neal asked annoyingly. "He just stood there after he opened the chest and instead of throwing it, he just froze and said, 'Fuck'. Now I have to clean brain matter off the walls while he clocks out of there." Neal moaned as crumbs of eggs and toast fell onto his tray.

Adam took a swig of milk and scratched his head.

"Well, it's not like we haven't all been there. Maybe he wanted out like we did," Adam said solemnly. Neal sank his head low. "The lucky bastard got away though," he retorted.

Adam looked over in confusion.

"He didn't have a capsule copy?" Adam asked.

"Nah, forgot to mention, he was some bigwig who knew a little too much about this place. Rumor is the doctor's taking some heat from foreign countries that are at war. Guess the guy thought he could strong arm the doctor for some assistance."

Adam's eyebrows rose.

"Must have had a big pair of balls for him to do that."

Adam chuckled.

"An army of clones," Neal said, shuddering at the thought. "As far as the word goes, no one's come close to perfecting RNA memory transfers. The doctor just hoards his research and on occasion, will give out encrypted reports with not much in 'em," Neal said.

He spread more butter on his toast.

Adam shook his head.

"What country would even want it? You can't artificially speed up the growth process for clones; they'd have to wait in real time, preserving and maintaining a platoon of would-be soldiers. Would just be a waste of resources. Without memory transfers, the clones would be useless, dead in the water with debt for crying out loud," Adam responded.

Neal laughed. "Well, maybe you lack the imagination."

Adam rolled his eyes. "So, they come here, hit the place, grab the research and start memory transferring random civilians with soldier combat training?"

Neal shrugged, chugging down his milk.

"If they did, they'd still be straight outta luck. Can't have more than two personas, I get that, but I still see why they'd want to take it," Neal said, wiping away the crumbs off the table.

"Neal," Adam said sheepishly. "You know I never really apologized to you about—"

"Dude, we're in hell. It happens and frankly, I needed the break," he said laughing meekly. Wiping his hands on his shirt, Neal looked over to Adam and smirked. "Well, duty calls."

He wandered away to attend to his daily tasks.

"Duty calls, indeed," Adam said, wiping the food off of his mouth onto a sleeve.

***

After another long day of keeping the facility's needs met, Adam sat down on his bed, contemplating his next request sheet as he sipped the wine he had found on his desk. He looked at the television mounted on his side wall, turning it on and off without any media playing.

He did this for hours, sipping his wine and pressing the power button on his remote continually. Finally, he relinquished himself to his bed and slept. The images came and went depending on the night, Samantha and her family staring at him blankly, and Claire outstretching her hand but failing to reach him.

Atreus was revealing himself in different forms, decayed or still intact.

Sometimes, it was Gale of all people, barking orders at Adam to release him—as if Adam had any control over Gale's life. He didn't even have control over his own.

He could end himself. The thought occurred to him daily. As Claire said, it wasn't as if he would wake up again. The clone would be the one dealing with the doctor's lunacy.

He could simply resign himself to the darkness and pass the buck to his unlucky counterpart, again and again until the doctor ran out of resources or gave up.

Then again, the doctor could simply transfer part of his memories before he came to this thought process, and it would be a tireless and endless escapade of fragmented memories.

No, to kill himself once more would surely make things much worse for the next one. *Enough is enough. Give in,* he thought to himself.

He pretended the screams of the deceased were some sort of macabre lullaby given to him by the darkness. It made things easier as he faded into a deep sleep.

***

Being woken up by an alarm by his bedside brought him back from his state of nothingness. He washed himself thoroughly and dressed in his uniform. Stepping outside, the doctor was greeting him in the flesh after all this time. *A year and some change,* he thought.

Excitedly, the doctor motioned his hands toward his chest. "Come along now, Adam. Soon, so very soon, you'll learn to love this. It becomes a part of you. Teaching, guiding, and penalizing," the doctor said in an ominous tone. They passed several patient holding cells until they reached one with the patient's name registered as Billy.

"Well, this is your stop," the doctor stated with glee, pointing at the watch on his wrist. "I'll contact you on the other side!" Adam's soulless expression did not faze the doctor one bit, and he walked into the room without a word, like a scene from the past.

The cage, the sheet of white all around, and finally the patient strapped to the bed being bombarded with bright lights and a rotating fan all dug deep into Adam, but he did not show it. He refused to show that he cared. To the right of him was a cart and a cloche covering a hot plate. Adam opened the cart's drawers. Cleaning supplies, key cards, snacks, and even an electrical rod similar to the one Sevant had used long ago.

"Hello?" Billy called out in fear. "Is anyone there?"

Adam Looked at Billy from afar behind the metal bars. His eyes were a shimmering green, his jawline slightly less defined and rounder than Adam's.

A bit plumper, but overall, out of all the clones he'd met with different genetic combinations, this one was nearly the spitting image of himself.

Adam rolled his eyes. "Is he the one taking the test, or am I?" Adam said in an angered fashion. He opened the gate and noticed Billy struggling to turn his head that had been strapped down tightly. He pushed the cart in and grabbed the only chair.

Now, he was sitting at the other end of the cage.

After fifteen minutes of hearing Billy plead and beg for him to let him go free, the doctor's voice came on. "I'm afraid he won't do that unless, of course, I say so. So, I suggest you speak clearly and respectfully when I ask you this one question."

Billy's eyes welled up with tears as he attempted to nod back to the doctor.

"Good, good. Now, my dear Billy. Are you willing to follow all my instructions to the letter?"

"Of course! Of course! Just get me out of here."

Adam felt revolted by the scene, wishing the patient had a bit more spine. Then he realized that he had no room to criticize; he had been just the same back in the beginning.

He rubbed the temples of his forehead with both hands.

"Adam. Please, if you would release the young man." Adam quietly walked over to Billy, trying not to make eye contact as Billy stood upright on the bed.

"Thank you so much! Where am I? And do you have food?"

Adam sighed and looked Billy in the eyes.

"Listen to me carefully," Adam said in an ominous tone. "Whatever happens, nothing is personal. Neither of us has a choice in the matter. So please, just fall in line and do what the doctor requests of you. It'll only be worse for you if you even so much as breathe the wrong way." Billy nodded in silence as Adam pushed the cart nearer.

The doctor's grin reached the tips of his ears as he saw the events unfold.

"Now, Billy. You are going to have to eat since you're so hungry, am I right?" the doctor asked. Billy nodded in agreement, grabbing the glass of water on the cart and chugging it down.

Scratching his head out of concern, Adam picked up the cloche covering Billy's meal.

Huh, so that's why he had an extra sector help out with the farming yesterday, Adam thought, shaking his head in disapproval. Sitting on the plate were worms writhing and wiggling, attempting to grovel off the plate but upon closer inspection, they had been drenched in edible glue. Stuck to the plate, the worms continued struggling to break free.

Billy's hand covered his mouth in disgust.

"If you do not finish this plate within twenty minutes, I will have Adam here penalize you with a few good blows to the head. Do you understand?" the doctor asked in a playful tone. Billy, though completely revolted, seemed much more docile and tamer.

He didn't argue with the doctor, just cried as he stabbed the worms with his fork, unable to place it in his mouth. Adam saw himself in Billy, feeling every thought, every sensation.

"I know what it's like." Adam spoke softly. Billy looked up with tears in his eyes.

"I just can't do it," Billy said, shaking in fear.

Adam pushed Billy's hand toward his mouth as if pleading with him.

"Just close your eyes, and chomp down as hard as you can. Chomp and swallow. That's it," Adam said reassuringly. This back and forth went on until finally, Billy's courage grew slightly, and he started eating. Adam felt humble and moved at the same time.

Perhaps in a very sick way, he could mentor Billy and prevent him from making the same mistakes he did. To Adam's horror, he heard a loud beep within the room.

The time was up, and Billy had only just started to eat.

"You ungrateful rat!" the doctor screamed into the intercom. "You will eat what I provide, and you will thank me. If not, why not taste a bit of Adam's knuckles?"

Billy's eyes widened.

"No, please wait, I can finish it. I can finish it," Billy pleaded.

Adam's fist gave a swift and carefully placed uppercut against Billy's chin.

He was attempting to make his movements more theatrical to please the doctor as well as to relatively keep Billy unharmed.

Unaware of Adam's mercy, Billy simply wailed as he phased in and out of consciousness.

"Again," the doctor yelled in passion.

Adam directed his fist below Billy's ribcage, hitting the fattiest part of his body.

It had knocked the wind out of Billy but again, there were no sustainable injuries.

"Hit him more in his face, Adam!"

Billy's eyes opened momentarily as he could see Adam's knuckles in plain view, his fist crashing onto the top of his forehead.

"Again, Adam. This time, avoid the same spot and aim to break his silly nose!"

Then Adam went in for another blow as if Billy had become a punching bag, trying to make the doctor believe he was giving it his all.

"Stop! Enough is enough, my dear boy. I think he gets the picture," the doctor said in approval. Adam straightened himself and helped straighten Billy upright in front of the plate.

"Are you OK?" Adam asked in concern.

"No!" Billy yelled with tears in his eyes.

"You're fine," Adam stated, rolling his eyes and shaking his head once more.

Day by day, this was the routine—more tests, more penalties. It was like a dance of showmanship. Making grand gestures, screaming loudly but all in all, the injuries were minimal.

After each test, Adam would carefully attend to Billy's wounds and constantly gave him advice with regard to coping within this facility. Billy soon caught on.

He could see Adam struggle as he dealt out electrical shocks or had to beat him repeatedly. Adam grew more and more disgusted with himself and even more so with Sevant each day he saw him. He could barely keep it together. Yet Sevant was clearly at peace, without a shred of remorse. Apparently, the doctor was even bragging about

Adam in front of Sevant.

They had tapes recorded and shared among the other nurses.

"That was a nice right hook yesterday." Someone patted Adam on the back. "I could have sworn that was mine!" Sevant laughed boldly.

Adam shrugged, said thanks and walked away.

Neal could sense Adam's frustration and looked him dead in the eyes as they crossed paths in the facility. He pulled Adam to the side and spoke freely within a storage closet.

"Listen, I can see it. You're gonna break. It's not your fault and it isn't his. It's all down to the doctor. And word through the grapevine is he has a special test for Billy. If he fails, well, let's just say you're gonna have to hold out and not give in," Neal said with concern.

Adam nodded and thanked Neal for his concern.

He pushed his cart along the hall and opened Billy's cell door, leading him to the next test area. "The overall goal is simple, really. Kill one of these poor fools, or all three will die."

Billy had had enough and began hurling out expletives upon expletives toward the doctor.

"I wish I could see your stupid face so I could smash it with a tire iron, you crazy fuck! I'm not killing anyone today, or tomorrow, or the following day. You can go fuck yourself, you piece of shit!" Billy yelled out triumphantly.

"Adam, if you will, please," the doctor asked plainly and without any show of emotion.

Adam took out the Berretta and fired three clean shots into the captives, and Adam sighed in relief, knowing that their suffering had finally come to a close. However, Billy's mind shattered.

He fell to his knees and clawed at his face while tears dripped off his cheeks.

"Oh God! Why? Oh my God, why? Why are you fucking doing this?"

Billy screamed in torment. Almost completely ignoring him, Adam simply stared at the Berretta, thinking how sweet the sensation of death truly was.

"Adam!" the doctor yelled, attempting to gain his attention.

As if suddenly broken from a trance, Adam stood straight and listened carefully.

"Strap him into the chair. It's time for his penalty."

Adam walked over to Billy, pointing the gun at him and motioning it toward the chair located at the end of the room. Billy taunted Adam and roared with resolute vigor.

"Go ahead, fucking do it. End it all for me, asshole! You're as bad as that cocksucker!"

Without hesitation, Adam fired the gun, aiming at the outer layer of Billy's inner thigh.

The bullet grazed the thigh, drawing blood but missing the vital arteries.

Billy banged his balled-up fist against the floor. "Fuck, that hurts. It hurts so damn much!" Billy said, whining like an injured animal.

"Just get onto the chair. Please, just do it," Adam said with a worn-out expression, every fiber of him willing stubborn Billy to follow orders and just do what would be best for him.

Billy was more stubborn than he'd ever been, simply curling into a ball like an armadillo.

Adam placed the gun on the cart and dragged him by the legs toward the chair. All the while, Billy begged for mercy, clawing at the floor.

"No, please no! Just stop it! Stop it!" Billy cried.

Adam successfully strapped him down even though Billy thrashed and struggled about.

"Cut off more than one finger, Adam. Show him what happens when he defies my orders!" The doctor spoke in a condescending fashion.

Adam pushed the cart next to themselves while he took out a towel and rolled it gently.

"Billy, I need you to bite down on the rag." At first, Billy refused but as he noticed Adam begrudgingly pulling the long-bladed secateurs from the cart, he bit onto it with all his might.

"I'm going to cut two of them, OK," Adam said reassuringly.

Billy kept twisting his wrists and wiggled his fingers so that Adam could not get a hold of them. As Billy hyperventilated on the rag and his saliva dripped from the corner of his lips, Adam looked him squarely in the face.

"If you don't calm down, I'm going to cut more by accident," he said, worried.

Billy finally relented and closed his eyes.

Adam sharpened the edge of both blades as best he could, secretly palming a pain-relieving gel from the cart—one he had taken from the medical ward for an occasion such as this.

"Think of it as a marriage between flesh and metal. A bonding session," Adam spoke softly.

He snapped the first finger with ease. It was the pinky after all and initially, Billy was as still as a rock. However, he no longer had a fortified will. Billy rocked on the chair back and forth, screaming into the rag, shaking his head in fury, looking upon Adam with hatred-filled eyes.

Adam struggled to secure his hand in place, begging Billy to stop with the rocking.

Adam's second attempt was not so clean since Billy's movements were frenetic.

As he attempted to cut one more finger, the jolt in Billy's wrist shook Adam's balance, cutting not only into the ring finger but the middle and index as well.

Billy's eyes were filled with mad hysteria as the only fingers now on his left hand were his thumb and a dangling index finger. The doctor's voice echoed into the test area in a loud vibration, delivering the unmistakable, menacing, maniacal laughter of a deranged madman.

"I told you to stay as still as possible. Believe it or not, I'm trying to help you here, Billy," Adam said with regret in his voice.

He turned to the cart to grab some medical supplies to stop the bleeding.

"Marry this, asshole!" Billy shrieked as his right hand broke free from all his jostling. The moment flashed by in an instant. Adam could no longer control his body. In retrospect, if he could have done anything differently, he wished he'd just simply taken the bullet instead of following his body's instincts. Billy had reached for the gun on top of the cart.

Yet as he pulled the trigger, Adam's left hand pushed Billy's right arm away from himself. Billy fired the gun, the bullet struck the air and then lost itself into the white-walled room.

In contrast, Adam's right hand was baptized by Billy's blood as the secateurs penetrated into the left side of Billy's neck and escaped outwards from its right side.

Billy's eyes blinked softly in confusion. He tried to speak, but the only sound coming out was the gurgling of his throat pushing the blood out of all the crevices of his neck.

His head slumped over like a hammer striking a hot anvil.

Billy was dead and Adam would now have another voice added to his *lullaby*.

Adam removed the knife embedded in Billy's neck. The blood flowed out like honey, oozing slowly yet continually for a while until the heart had stopped beating for ten or more seconds.

Grabbing a body bag out from the cart, he lay it evenly on the floor, lifting his counterpart and placing him inside the bag. As he pulled the zipper to a close, all Adam could think of was the hatred-filled glare still present in Billy's dead eyes.

He cleaned the room until there was no trace of the travesty left, all evidence scrubbed away until the next episode, no doubt bringing another addition to the constantly changing lullaby.

Dragging the body bag by the door, Adam could hear footsteps from the other side. The door opened, revealing two men looking nothing like himself or the other myriad of clones.

A tall man towered well past the door frame, well-built and chiseled features unlike any Adam had ever seen before. His skin was that of a charcoal color, so dark that the brightness of plain white that the room gave off could not blot out this man's presence.

The other man was shorter; not pale, but of a slight amber complexion.

His eyes were sharp like those of a fox. While his stature seemed rather meek, his presence gushed forth, expressing wisdom and untapped knowledge.

The dark man laughed with a loud deep bellow and looked at Adam's face in amusement.

"You look like a deer in headlights!" the dark man said.

Adam was still stunned at seeing not one, but two human beings looking so drastically different from the ones he dealt with on a day-to-day basis.

"The name's Simon," the dark man said. "This one over here is Peter. He's quiet most of the time but don't let that fool ya. Two glasses of good Scotch and you can't get him to shut up."

Peter rolled his eyes and stooped, picking up the other half of the body.

He helped Adam to lift it.

"All right," the doctor said. "You needed some help, so come on, second class." Walking down the hall with Peter and Simon, Adam finally grew the courage to speak.

"Who are you two?" he asked inquisitively.

"We're your seniors, little buddy," Simon said with a hint of sarcasm. They reached a dump chute and dropped the body free of ceremony.

Adam looked upon the two gentlemen, finding them a stark contrast from each other in appearance and personality, yet he could see a peculiar sort of kinship.

Unbeknownst to Adam, they had a bond that had lasted for centuries, a deal long struck between them and the doctor.

"Have there been any other first-class nurses before you two?" Adam asked, wiping his hands with an antiseptic.

Peter looked at Simon, and Simon met his gaze.

In sequence, they laughed sheepishly.

"No, not at all," Peter responded.

Simon pointed his finger at Adam with a stern look.

"And that stays between US!" Simon's tone was firm yet relaxed. "You only get to know because we're bringing you into the fold so to speak."

"Into the fold!" Peter added with a jolly pep in his step.

Adam simply marveled at the two. They were so different, lively and filled with personality.

"Are you two clones?" Adam asked.

Peter sighed, looking at Simon. "Does it even matter if we talk to him?"

"Not really. Once the transfer's complete, he will know everything." They both laughed almost menacingly.

A fox and a wolf, Adam thought as he could tell these two nurses were above it all. Above the menial tasks of third and second-class nurses, even above the doctor's influence.

Are they on equal terms? Adam's thoughts continued to cycle until the three came upon a large metal door, sealed shut with three scanners to gain entry.

Simon moved his head close to the door, staring directly into one scanner, opening his mouth for the second and placing his whole right hand on the third.

A loud hissing noise came from the seams of the door as a cool breeze blew into Adam's face.

Simon and Peter stepped on opposing sides to the entrance, both waving a guiding hand.

"Go on," they stated in sequence, all the while chuckling as if they knew something Adam was not privy to. Obediently, Adam walked into the dim room until the door slid back into place, permanently locking him in, cocooning him in the darkness that forebode his final resting place.

Adam slowly walked forward toward the brightest light source in the room, passing vat after vat of clone bodies in suspended animation, each one giving off a very dim light of yellow.

Mixed in with the regular clones were those of Simon and Peter, the vats for these clones labeled VIP. Adam rolled his eyes as he continued inspecting the clones.

They would twitch and move eerily, as if all stuck in a nightmare, contorting and shaking every so often, awaiting the day they opened their eyes to this Godforsaken place.

Eventually, Adam reached a table with an old flickering computer box sitting atop it, the screen phasing in and out with streams of code running along its surface.

The mouse and keyboard were weathered, collecting dust from disuse.

"This is our clone storage facility," the doctor said, stepping out from the darkness behind the table. In a moment, the room lit up and all of the doctor's life's work lay there before Adam.

It was a much larger computer setup, with varying displays of the whole facility. Monitors showed copious data top to bottom such as genetic code structures, trials, and the personal info of each patient. Characteristics, choices, mental state... It was all there, each opposing side of the room filled with even more vatted clones.

There must be hundreds upon hundreds of clones in here, Adam thought.

The doctor waved his hand to a machine just off the side of the display monitors. Adam reluctantly sat on the chair and awaited further instructions.

The doctor was pleased with this and spoke endearingly. "Worry not, my dear boy. Soon, all will be revealed. If you stay as docile as this, there will be no issue with the transfer."

Adam simply sat quietly. However, in his mind, he steeled himself.

No matter what happens, he thought, *I will still be me.*

The doctor strapped a silver device to Adam's head, its image resembling that of a crown, with many protruding spikes connecting to an array of colored cables. He then strapped Adam into the chair firmly, so much so that Adam could feel his blood flow nearly lose its circulation.

The doctor hesitated for a moment, looking over at Adam once more.

"To living forever," he stated as he pressed a key on the far more advanced computer. The lights were flickering on and off as a loud humming gradually grew in volume.

"You see, my dear boy!" the doctor yelled, attempting to communicate through the loud noise. "The longer we live, the more information is stored. Three hundred years of memories and knowledge is about to flow into you. I do not envy you for this process will most likely break you down to your very core. However, this is not the end!"

The whirling and screeching of the machine almost drowned out the doctor's voice.

"Our new beginning!" he screamed in ecstasy, raising his hands to the air, tears welling.

"Remember! Remember it all!"

Adam's eyes rolled into his skull, his teeth grating and his ears spilling blood.

His body, although the doctor had strapped it down completely, still shook uncontrollably.

His mouth began foaming and his voice howled like a mad dog.

Streams and streams of light were flooding his mind, each passing ray showing snippets of scenes of a forgotten past… His high school days with Peter and Simon, their college years studying memory RNA and vowing to live forever, being the first humans to have defeated death itself. He saw a much older Claire walking in the halls of their school and then years later, her giving him a cup of coffee as she returned to their bedroom.

He could feel the intense long hours of research and toiling away with the math and application of it all. He saw Simon and Peter finding little to no information worth any value, not until Claire solved the equation by accident, erasing two numbers on the board, attempting to stop him from his work. Adam could see his hand stopping hers in place before she erased the rest. The answer to death's foul dealings was in front of him the whole time.

He rejoiced and called his colleagues over to start applying trial runs.

Claire, visibly frustrated, held back her misgivings.

He could see this, and Adam took her by her hand.

"My love, when this is over, we will live together forever and ever."

She laughed solemnly and looked Adam in his tired eyes.

"We are here now and will die later or the next you or me will be completely different people once they make new memories of their own." She looked at Adam sternly. "You and I are soulmates," she said with conviction. "We will see one another on the other side. You helped me break away from my darkness, so let me prevent you entering your own."

Adam could feel the anger and resentment welling up inside himself.

"You murdered and slaughtered over fifty men for their past sins, gutted them like pigs and burned their flesh when you were done with them!" Adam screeched. "You want to lecture me for giving a gift to humanity?" He was flabbergasted.

Claire calmly stroked his cheeks.

"That's not me anymore," she said in peace. "This thing you have been working toward could cause a lot of good, yes, but it could also be used for evil. I wouldn't want my next self to see you spiral out of control. Please let us die and move on when the time comes."

She was crying.

"Give your research to someone else and let *them* bear the burden, not us," Claire said.

Adam relented and kissed her, never broaching the subject again.

The memories continued to flood inside of Adam's brain, years upon years of sheer emotion. He could feel pleasure, hate, fear, joy, and even the self-doubt of continuing his research.

***

Simon and Peter diligently worked long into the night.

Human trials would be the next step, and with all their arrogance and pride on the line, they each took their own DNA and began breeding their very first clones.

Adam then stored all three of their memory sets in three separate small capsules.

Once stored, the memories slowed as he homed in on the memory of their death together, he and Claire. She held him as tight as she could, her age apparent. Her teeth were all but gone, hair white as chalk and her once beautiful voice replaced by withered breathing and tired mutterings.

Claire's old hand touched Adam's face as they both stared into each other's eyes.

Hers were a beautiful blue, a stark contrast to his green. Even in dying, her eyes were still brimming with life, still holding the power to melt Adam's soul for Adam belonged to her and Claire knew that she belonged to him likewise. It was a good life, not perfect in any regard, but a life well lived. Sons and daughters. Grandkids and old friends. What more could one ask for?

Let death come with open arms because in the end, life's only meaning comes from the warmth you feel from others, a meaning that cannot be taken but only given by the joy you spread. This is life's true meaning, Adam thought.

The truth was she had cancer and was destined to die in the few days to come, but what of it?

Should she whimper in fear of death?

Even if there awaited nothing but a black abyss, there was still beauty in a life lived, a story shared between two lovers, and a grand tale with sorrow and joy. After sixty years of matrimony, they were ready. A man stood above them; he was their caretaker.

"Are you both ready?" the man asked.

"Yes, I believe we are," Claire said. "What a knockout!" She giggled at the man.

Adam chuckled, rolling his eyes. "I'm right here, you know," he said comically.

"Well, how would you explain that?" She pointed at the man.

Adam looked at the man and sighed.

"That is the ghost of the man I once was. Afraid of death and unwilling to broaden my views on the world." The man did not respond but took a syringe and fed both their intravenous lines with a large dose of morphine. And he waited.

As they shared a passionate kiss, Claire peacefully welcomed death, her eyes dying while looking upon the eyes of her one true love. Adam followed suit but was feeling a burning sensation at the back of his neck, barely perceptible but still there, taking all of his might, turning his head while still holding Claire's hand. There, the man was standing triumphantly with a capsule unbeknownst to Adam. His eyes widened when the realization hit him.

The clone snickered with menacing joy.

"When you decided to play doll house, your brothers in arms decided to use the transfer on your clone. Of course, I pretended to just be the humble servant with no recollection of a past."

Adam's mouth was agape, holding out his hand, reaching for the capsule.

He grabbed the clone's wrist with all the might he could muster.

Then there was nothing but silence. Adam had died.

"Tsk, tsk, tsk, old man," the clone said as he pulled away from the feeble man's grasp.

The clone walked over to a mirror placed above their dresser, then he spoke to the mirror.

"You know what I have always hated? You got to be with our true love while I, still having all the recollection of our past life, had to stay and continue on with the research.

"To be honest, I don't care that you had no idea, and I don't care that Simon and Peter went along with it against your wishes. The fact is, I did not get to be my own man. I am now you.

"Well, I am the you who never gave up on his research. The you who had the stones to do what was necessary. So, I implanted the capsules into both of you."

The clone pointed at the two corpses with his thumb, still staring daggers at the mirror.

"You get to die, of course, but I'm not letting you go entirely."

The clone stood there looking at himself, swaying his pointer finger back and forth.

"You see, while you were enjoying our best life, I found a few workarounds against the kinks of merging memories from one person to another when they already have memories of their own.

"If the transferred memories pass into a body of a similar genetic makeup, the survival rate goes from zero percent to about sixty-two. Give or take," he said with a mocking tone.

"There is so much to do and we have very many backers at our disposal now. An endless stream of revenue if you will, and I just recently got into real estate. Hope you like coconuts!"

The clone laughed. The memories flooded in, deeper and faster.

He could see the clone market his idea to other nations, attending scientific seminars, stealing research while Simon and Peter assisted with clinical trials on civilians, finding that fear, trauma, and pain were ideal motivators for long-lasting memories.

All the atrocities he had ever committed laid themselves bare and open in Adam's core. He saw it all, hundreds of years of torture and debauchery, nearly too much to bear.

The guilt preceded by the revolution could never be contained.

Adam reeled back into the seat, still convulsing and his mouth foaming, his eyes still hiding in desperation inside of his skull.

His mouth snapped wide as he vomited all over his extremities, copious and odorous.

The putrid liquid would not cease, spewing forth until his body completely shut down.

His mind once more faded off into the abyss.

As his mind drifted into the darkness, he could hear his own voice cackling, echoing all across the expanse of nothingness, a demonic laughter continuing and growing louder until finally, tendrils within the darkness slowly formed. The entity rapidly spewed blood from the lower parts of its tentacles, pushing out the crown of a naked body's head.

The darkness was bleeding, giving birth to a new abomination, the laughter turning to screams, but not the screams of his own. They were the screams of his victims, damning him to hell, wishing that this abomination's existence be erased from all four corners of the earth, thousands upon thousands of souls screaming in anguish and hatred.

The blood gushed out of the tendrils as they deflated and became flaccid.

Like a foul beast excreting excrement, the head popped out and then finally, the rest of the body as a loud thud rang in the ether.

"Hello there, Adam, or should I just say, hello me?" the newborn creature said with a gnarly smile. It was the spitting image of himself, and it made Adam's heart rend.

Immediately, the creature latched onto Adam as its hands began merging into his skin and bone. All the while, Adam screamed in agony and lunacy.

"Stop, dear God, why? Stop!"

"Sh, sh, sh, sh, sh. It's almost over."

The creature bit into Adam, sucking and licking his neck.

"Sooooooo gooooood!" the creature cried out, and Adam could feel his own self, his very soul fading away and merging into the new Adam's soul, wanting to relent but holding on out of sheer fear of losing himself to this thing who he knew was the doctor.

"I'm not going to become the next serial murderer in line!"

Slowly though, not noticeably at first, Adam pushed back against the doctor's soul.

"Just give in to it, you fool," the doctor screeched within his head.

"I will not let you win. You have to lose!" Adam declared.

"I have always claimed victory since the day we killed us!"

"You can't keep doing this to us and to others who aren't even a part of this. You can't!" Adam cried out in opposition, two personas in a battle for supremacy, each no longer relenting their stake of the body in which it resided.

"There is nothing you can do now, Adam! I'll have this body, and your memories will be absorbed into mine!" In the darkness, a bright light cut across before them in an instant.

From the light, Adam could see Claire, Atreus and Neal reaching out with their hands.

Adam grabbed on as they pulled him farther and farther away into the light. A loud cry of hatred and malice was echoing in the darkness as the doctor's soul grabbed onto Adam's legs.

"This is what I was afraid of," the doctor snarled. "Outside influences of other memories! Do know, fool, that if you don't succeed, you will die entirely. Simply give in, and a small portion of your self will lie dormant within me, and you could enjoy the darkness's warm embrace forever!"

Claire's face smiled as Atreus smirked and Neal chuckled.

They all looked back to the doctor with a triumphant demeanor.

"No deal," they said as the arms holding Adam ripped off, still holding onto Adam's ankles. Adam's eyes opened, adjusting to the light. Still strapped to the chair, the doctor stood before Adam holding a nine-millimeter Berretta, pointed at Adam's head.

"Did the transfer work?" the doctor asked.

Adam mimicked the cold-hearted smile he saw within his headspace.

"Of course, it worked," Adam replied.

"Then answer me this one question. What is our true name?"

Adam, perplexed and exhausted from the whole process, could barely sum up the words. Yet just as the doctor's finger came to pulling the trigger, he heard Claire's voice.

"Enoch, your name is Enoch!"

Adam looked at the doctor with a pompous attitude.

"Enoch, you damn oaf. I don't care to think of it in the first place," Adam said in deceit.

"Good."

The doctor placed the gun on the table beside Adam and began loosening the straps.

"May I remind you that after this procedure, we still have to…"

Bang! A loud cracking sound filled the room. The doctor cursed and swore in pain as Adam had just shot him on his right knee.

"How is this possible? This has never happened before! We always transfer with great success." The doctor curled into the fetal position, covering his face. "Don't shoot, please don't shoot!" the doctor begged in tears, his face red as he groveled on the floor like a scared child.

"Nothing matters, you fool!" the doctor cried out. "I can give meaning to this world! We can do great things, you and I! You'd throw that all away for revenge?"

The doctor's voice was unsteady and weak.

The words slipping out of his mouth slurred, drenched in fear.

Adam smiled and laughed the same cackling laughter he heard within his mind.

"I can still feel him trying to break out and help you," Adam said coldly. "I'll admit, you almost had me too." *Bang!* Another shot, the bullet tackling the doctor's other kneecap.

The doctor cried, clawing at the floor, dragging himself to a table near the old computer.

"You see this thing here? It might appear meaningless at first glance, but I use this computer for one thing and one thing only! If I die, a transmitter in my body sends a signal to it, and if no one inputs the passcode within the next two minutes, this whole facility burns in the flames of hell! A sixty-megaton blast destroying this island and destroying anything that could even see the explosion in the first place. It's all over, Adam."

The doctor's laughter betrayed his insanity.

Adam responded with the same laughter and followed with a remorseless retort.

"One thing, Doctor. I think we both know I am not afraid to die. And two, who said anything about killing you?" The doctor, still crying and with a mottled pink face, looked at Adam and realized who he was talking to.

"Enoch?" the doctor asked.

"Yes, Adam?" Enoch replied.

"How?" the doctor cried out.

Enoch squatted closer to the doctor and looked him dead in the eyes.

"You were playing with fire the minute you decided to merge my memories with yours." The doctor was thrown into a fit of rage as he banged his head repeatedly against the table.

"Had I known my memories were inside of you, I would have killed you. Your memories came from the height of my career as a scientist. Claire hadn't yet influenced me the way she did all those years ago. You are my ego, my avarice, and Claire has always been my Conscience.

"When Simon and Peter stored my memory RNA, I asked them to get rid of it years later.

"I even deleted the files off my private server just in case but instead, I assume they had a backup copy. I thought if a clone of myself lived on, it would bring no harm since they could choose the life they wanted to live," Enoch said in a calm manner.

The doctor pulled on his lab coat, shaking it furiously. "But this is not the future I choose now, is it!"

"I know."

Enoch paused for a moment, digging deep within himself to find common ground with his wayward creation. "I know, and for that I am truly sorry," he stated with a cool head. "That being said, parts of the doctor, Adam, and Enoch are all swimming around in here now."

He pointed at his forehead. "I have Adam's resilience, and my God, was he resilient. I have his naivete and want of vengeance. I have the doctor's bloodlust, intellect, and lunacy.

"Then I have Enoch's compassion, empathy, and hope, all combined and intertwined. So, part of me wants to help you while the other wants to kill you. All the while, I have to be the judge between the doctor and the new Adam." Enoch looked at the doctor coldly. "Why go through all of this when it could have been done in a sane and safe manner?"

The doctor looked into Enoch's eyes and spat in his face. "Because I could!"

"Interesting, but wrong answer," Enoch said with a blank expression.

Bang! The bullet pierced through the doctor's right arm, leaving it limp. He cried out in hysteria, "It was because I brought that bitch, wasn't it? This is all her fault, you leaving your research and Adam's fortitude against the transfer!"

Enoch nodded in agreement.

"Mostly true. Why did you do it then, you old fool?" he gave a soft chuckle.

"I wanted to prove she was meaningless just like the rest of the world! To prove to myself that even with her intervention, my true self would never give up on my research, on my glory!"

"Well, she proved you wrong, didn't she?" Enoch replied.

The doctor fell silent, looking at the ground in disdain.

"You just wanted to see her, didn't you? You wanted to love her again, so you used Adam to show her your love." The doctor's left fist smashed against the back side of the table.

"Enough!" the doctor yelled out. "They're here already."

Simon and Peter were rushing in, attempting to save the doctor, but it was too late.

"Atreus sends his regards!" *Bang!*

The final bullet pierced the doctor's skull, leaving a satisfying smile on Enoch's face.

Simon and Peter clutched their heads and ran off to the computer in hopes of stalling the detonation. Alarms throughout the facility began ringing.

"Fuck, fuck, fuck, fuck!" Simon yelled, working on the computer diligently.

Peter, completely in shock, fell to his knees. Enoch laughed once more and saw his old colleagues looking at them fondly, yet disappointed.

"What happened to you two? You guys were so bright and so brilliant. Why would you let this happen?" Simon slammed the table with the palm of his hand with tremendous force.

"Because you were too chickenshit to do what had to be done!" Simon screamed in full force. Peter shook his head in disapproval. "You left us and our dreams for some girl, Enoch."

Enoch's eyes drooped downwards for a moment in recollection.

"I fell in love with her. Was that a crime?" Enoch yelled in retort.

"You left us with a homicidal maniac of a clone!" Simon said in justification. "He would never have gotten like that had you not transferred my old memories into him!"

"You did little to stop him," Enoch replied.

"He threatened us the moment this place was rigged to blow, started acting like hot shit and took over everything!" Peter said in anger.

Still holding the gun in one hand, Enoch went over to the computer and pressed in the passcode. The siren of the alarm lowered in intensity and frequency.

Simon and Peter dropped to the floor in relief.

"Go tell all the nurses and patients it's over. Evacuate the place if you can." Simon and Peter looked at each other, confused. "I'd say you have about two hours to get on a plane by the shipyard and fly out of here."

"Didn't you stop the bomb?" Peter asked desperately.

"It has two-step authentication. The first code just buys you that amount of time. The doctor's persona within me is fighting me on this. He'd rather watch it all burn than have his original creator run the show. Now go," Enoch yelled.

The two bolted toward the exit. "For what it's worth, it was nice hearing from you again!" Peter called out. Simon simply shook his head, still sprinting to the exit.

Enoch monitored all the evacuees including Neal, seeing him enter in a frenzy while Simon and Peter entered the cockpit. As far as Enoch could tell, within the hour, the whole facility was devoid of any life but his own. He remembered his years here, remembered all the different Adams, Atreuses, and Neals. He remembered the innocent bystanders he had killed.

This was all a parade of death and screams for his own vanity. Enoch sat in the control seat for the facility, looking at the monitor screens filled with countless memories and pain.

He cried for the people he had killed, the people he'd saved, the people he had lost, and he cried for humanity as a whole. All it took was one man with a plan and with a snap of his fingers, he could cause so much torment.

He looked over to one of the vats in particular, knowing it was Claire.

He needed to make things right with her.

So, he looked up her memory files and compounded them with the ones she had at this facility. He stored everything Claire had seen, done, or had ever heard into a memory capsule.

Using an injection apparatus located within the vat's sealed cap, he injected the capsule at the base of her neck. Shortly after, she awakened and was none too pleased.

Clothed in the doctor's bloodied lab coat, she lashed out at him, screaming profanities and slapping him in the face several times.

As she cried, she looked into his eyes and kissed him with all her passion.

"I told you to give up on it," she stated.

"Claire, I did. I promise you I did. I didn't know that the clone had my memories!" Enoch retorted. Claire looked into his eyes, stern.

"You should never have made the clone in the first place," she said. They argued for a while more until it dawned on her. "Didn't you say this place is rigged to blow?"

Enoch laughed. "I may have fibbed a bit. I stopped it from going off; there was no other authentication process. I just left the alarm bells ringing," he stated.

They both laughed, unstoppable and like school kids, reminiscing over the times they had spent together. They cried and expelled all of their sorrows to one another.

All lies were rectified, and all secrets told.

They continued on and on for hours, all the while, Enoch knowing this would have to end.

"The world at large could never know about this place and its knowledge. Do you really believe there is more than just this life?" Enoch asked with doubt in his heart.

Claire smiled. "You already followed me into death once. Why not follow me again, and I'll show you?"

Enoch walked over to the old computer and typed in a code.

Music drifted forth from the main hub computer.

The Romance for Violin and Orchestra No. 2 in F Major, Op. 50. Her favorite.

Claire grabbed onto Enoch. "Not even death will keep us apart," she said in warmth.

"I set the timer to ten minutes," Enoch replied.

"Care to dance with me then?" Claire outstretched her hand in wait.

"Forever and always," Enoch replied.

As Enoch and Claire danced, Adam's persona took hold, and the Claire persona developed within the facility followed suit.

"These two have had their fun and a lifetime together, but it's our turn now," Claire said in conviction. Adam laughed and stared into her beautiful emerald-green eyes.

"Blue or green makes no difference to me," Adam said.

They gingerly danced in between the vats holding their various counterparts, a musical gallop between the lifeless and the life fulfilled.

Holding onto her hands, Adam wept in joy.

"A proper send-off, wouldn't you agree?" Claire said with her brilliant smile.

Adam nodded his head in agreement.

As the songs drew to a close, they stopped and held one another, sharing one last kiss of passion as the facility around them glowed in a blinding white light.